Grace

CHRIS KENISTON
USA TODAY BESTSELLING AUTHOR

Indie House Publishing

Indie House Publishing

BOOKS BY CHRIS KENISTON

Aloha Series
Aloha Texas
Almost Paradise
Mai Tai Marriage
Dive Into You
Shell Game
Look of Love
Love by Design
Love Walks In
Waikiki Wedding

Surf's Up Flirts
(Aloha Series Companions)
Shall We Dance
Love on Tap
Head Over Heels
Perfect Match
Just One Kiss
It Had to Be You

Honeymoon Series
Honeymoon for One
Honeymoon for Three

Family Secrets Novels
Champagne Sisterhood
The Homecoming
Hope's Corner

Farraday Country

Adam
Brooks
Connor
Declan
Ethan
Finn
Grace
Hannah
Ian
Jamison

ACKNOWLEDGEMENTS

Some books come easily, some are a little more difficult. The turning point writing *Grace* came thanks to the lovely people at Sheldon Feed in Elk Grove, California. Yeah, this Texas gal had to go all the way to California to find a good old-fashioned feed store. The gals let me walk around, take photos, and once Manager Susie figured out I wasn't some crazy woman on a mission (well, maybe I am but we won't tell her that), she showed me all around, roped in fellow employee Lindsay to answer more questions, and together they volunteered so much information I could hardly wait to get home and write more on Chase and his new career. Ladies, you rock!

I also have to thank my friends Kathy Ivan and Jana DeLeon (both fantastic authors). Kathy for letting me sprawl out on her way more comfortable than mine sofa, and Jana for sharing her primo chiropractor. Without the three of them I may never have finished *Grace*!

I know I'm forgetting so many people, but please know every nugget of an idea, every suggestion, every word of encouragement, every photo for inspiration are all appreciated more than words can express.

Please enjoy Grace and the rest of the Farraday clan and stick around for more fun when cousins Hannah, Ian, and Jamison come to town to play!

Enjoy!
Chris

P.S. All mistakes on life and work in West Texas are all mine and not the fault of my wonderful advisors.

CHAPTER ONE

Propping the alley door open, Chase Prescott looked left, then right. No sign of his new friend. Dropping another bag onto the pile, he would have loved to shut down, remodel, upgrade, and reopen his new business, but common sense told him that in this small market he could not afford to lose even one customer to inconvenience. Within a week of signing on the dotted line, before opening the doors to customers each day, Chase had been doing his best to get in a couple of hours work cleaning out decades of worthless merchandise. Putting out the trash on his second day at the job, he noticed a stealth dog lurking down the side alley.

Strong intelligent eyes had captured Chase's attention. Back in Manhattan, it seemed everyone he knew had small yappy dogs with polished toenails and ribbons atop their heads. Convinced this magnificent animal was foraging for food, Chase stepped inside and returned with a dish of leftover lunch only to find the dog had vanished as quickly as he'd appeared.

The following day, having drawn closer, the prowling animal paused to regard Chase, as though sizing him up, before moving on. This same ritual had become part of Chase's routine the last few days. Now almost time to lock up for the day, he wondered where his daily visitor was.

Peering around from behind the mountain of outdated dry goods along the alley wall, familiar amber eyes once again sized him up. "Have I not passed the test yet?" Chase crouched down on his haunches, waiting to see if today would be the day the dog would finally come close enough for him to check for any signs of ownership. Patiently balancing in place, he resisted the urge to fist pump the air when slowly the furry canine crept up in front of him.

Scanning the dog from head to rump, he searched for signs of injury or starvation. Though the fellow looked pretty lean, Chase suspected it had more to do with a high metabolism. "Somewhere," he held his hand, palm open, for the dog to sniff, "in your family tree, I'd bet there's been a wolf or two." *Or three.* Odd patches of color indicated his maternal ancestors had more than likely been cattle dogs. Maybe border collie. More comfortable of the animal's friendly nature, Chase raised his hand to scratch behind the dog's ears, surprised when he leaned his head into Chase's touch. "Okay, maybe I'm wrong. Maybe you do belong to someone."

The old-fashioned bell over the front doors sounded. Not the obnoxious *dong* of modern electronics, but the delicate jingle of an era long gone by. Slowly, Chase pushed to his feet. "Sorry boy, I've got to take care of business." Every time that sound rang, a shot of adrenaline spiked, propelling Chase eagerly forward. Who knew a stupid bell could be so exciting.

Four years at one of the best business schools in the country. Ten years on Wall Street making his mark on the world—and his bank account. Now the remainder of Chase's resume would be condensed to owner of a small-town farm and feed store—and God how he already loved everything about this place.

The local police chief filled the doorway with a tall man cut from the same cloth beside him. "Hey."

"Chief." Any other place or time and Chase would have assumed a visit from the local authority meant something somewhere had gone wrong. Very wrong. Here, he'd already learned, paying a social call was the norm.

"This isn't official business. Call me DJ."

"Very well. DJ it is."

DJ's almost-clone stuck out his hand. "Finn Farraday. Nice to meet you."

"Same here." Before agreeing to buy out the feed store, Chase had done some checking around and knew the Farradays owned one of the largest ranch operations in the county. From what little information Mr. Thomas had shared after the sale, the Farradays had always been one of the store's best customers.

"I see you're not changing the name?" Finn waved a thumb over his shoulder indicating the storefront behind him.

"Not—"

"Well, look who's here." DJ took a few steps forward and squatted down. With its tail wagging, the stray eagerly trotted up to him. "Don't you look happy." The police chief began a two handed under-the-neck rubdown. Had the dog been a cat, he'd be purring.

Grinning, Finn leaned over to scratch the dog's back then suddenly stopped, cocked his head, and squinted. "Does Gray look a little taller to you?"

Tilting his body back a bit, DJ shook his head. "Nope."

"You've got a nice dog." Chase thought the strong lithe dog suited the man.

"Not mine." DJ continued to stroke the animal.

Chase looked to Finn.

"Nope." Finn shrugged. "Not mine either."

"Hmm. Sure looks like he belongs to somebody."

"That's what we all thought." The chief patted the dog and stood upright. "If you figure out who he belongs to, make sure to let us know."

Chase nodded and wondered who *we all* referred to. "Sure thing."

"Well," Finn stretched out his hand again, "I just wanted to introduce myself and give you a welcome to town. I've been late getting around to it, but things have been a bit hectic." He sprouted a grin even wider than when he'd spotted the dog. "Just got myself engaged."

The pieces fell together. Staying at the B&B until he figured out long term housing of his own, Chase had heard a good deal about the Farradays. Already having met Adam, Meg's husband, and DJ, the police chief, it shouldn't have been such a surprise for Chase to discover the family resemblance extended to more of the siblings. Now he'd also been surprised to realize the strapping man in front of him was the recently engaged youngest brother. "Congratulations."

Frowning, DJ stepped aside. "Another door open?"

Chase nodded. "Yeah, that's how the dog followed me..." He looked around. "Where did he go?"

"That's what he does. Just disappears." Finn shook his head and took another step toward the rear.

The bell over the door sounded and, like a shooting star, Gray sprang up out of nowhere, bolted past the three men and lunged forward.

"Shit," three male voices echoed.

Visions of wolf fangs sinking deep into an unsuspecting customer had Chase sprinting after the animal. *Damn it*. Finn on his heels, Chase saw the chief reach for his holster and his heart skipped a beat. He didn't want to see the dog hurt, but friendly or not, strays could turn. Just what he needed. Less than a week in town and already Chase would be making front-page news for all the wrong reasons.

A loud howl pierced the panicked silence. In a simultaneous blur, a tall brunette closed the door behind her—arms stiff, DJ raised his gun toward the door—and the lightning-quick dog leapt up, knocking the lady off her feet and into a display of garden seeds.

Arms and legs flailing, packets flying left and right, the woman let out a stunned yelp. The police chief and his brother came to a stop silently on either side of her.

"What the...?" Rather than find a bloodied victim, Chase saw the dog standing over the prone woman, licking her face.

The two brothers burst into laughter. The chief holstered his gun and Finn turned, slapped Chase on the shoulder, and grinning, muttered, "Here we go again."

• • • •

Flat on her back, Grace took a few extra seconds to process what the hell had just happened. Eyes squeezed tight she finally figured out the new owner's dog was the reason her brothers were laughing at her. What she couldn't figure out was why in the name of all that was holy was the animal slobbering over her like a long lost relative. "Would someone please call Rover off of me?"

The man she assumed was the new owner of the feed store let out a piercing whistle. Much to her relief, the animal took off in his direction. At the same time, two arms appeared in front of her from either side.

"You okay, sis?" DJ's voice tumbled over Finn's.

On her feet and brushing off her clothes, her embarrassment, and the crash landing, Grace honed in on the man now escorting the furry beast out to the rear storage area. "You seriously need to teach that animal some manners."

DJ swallowed a smile, but Finn made no effort to hide his mirth.

"About that." Finn scanned her from head to toe, reassuring himself she was not injured, and folded his arms across his chest. "That's Gray."

Squinting in thought, she looked from Finn to DJ.

"The dog," DJ explained, as though she'd forgotten how to speak English.

"Should be penned where he can't hurt the customers." Even though her jeans held no sign of damage, she brushed at an imaginary speck of dust.

"No, sis," DJ repeated, "*the* dog."

"Whatever," she waved him off, turning to the direction the store owner was returning from, "all it takes to go out of business before you get started is for one customer to sue you for trying to kill them. One very pissed-off customer."

"In all fairness, before you speak," DJ looked to the store owner, "I should warn you. She's a lawyer."

"She hasn't taken the bar yet," Finn countered. "So technically…"

Grace shot her slightly older brother a venomous glare. Wasn't it bad enough she'd just taken a fall suitable for a slapstick vaudeville routine? She did not need her brother emphasizing technicalities. "I am a lawyer. And if you hadn't noticed, I have a sister-in-law who is not only an extremely skilled and feared litigator, she's licensed to litigate in Texas."

"She does have a point." DJ shrugged at his younger brother before looking to Chase.

"I am sorry—" Chase started.

"You should be." She cut off the attempted apology, brushing at an arm for good measure before waving over the mess beside her. "Your dog is a menace."

"Except he's not my dog." The man had an irritatingly appealing smile.

She didn't need to notice a good-looking man when she was spitting mad. Or his sparkling eyes. "Are you laughing at me?"

"No, ma'am." His eyes widened. "I'm just pointing out that I am not the owner of the dog."

Grace took a step forward and Finn slid in front of her. "We told you, sis. That's the dog."

Furious at her brother for blocking her path, it took longer than it should have for her to realize her siblings were trying to get a point across. One she was clearly missing.

With his right hand, DJ tapped on the ring finger of his left hand.

And she got it. "Oh, hell no." She spun on her heel and climbed over the splattered mess all around her.

"I think I'm missing something,." The store owner glanced from sibling to sibling.

Finn and DJ exchanged looks and smiles, followed by casual shrugs.

"Let's start with introductions." DJ looked to his sister. "Grace, this is Chase Prescott. He's the one who bought this place from old man Thomas." With a half spin in Chase's direction and a wave of his arm toward Grace, he continued. "And Chase, let me introduce you to my sister, Grace."

Finn chuckled. "And according to Gray, your future wife."

CHAPTER TWO

"I thought Grace and Finn would be back by now. Shall we play another hand?" Eileen shifted her attention from the view of Main Street to her friends of well over twenty years sitting at the table.

"I'm in." Dorothy picked up the deck to her side. "I wonder what's holding them up. Wasn't Finn just stopping in to meet Chase?"

"Well, the man is single." Sally May cut the deck.

Ruth Ann waved her hand under her chin. "Don't forget good looking."

"Very." Dorothy dealt the first cards. "Maybe he's caught Gracie's eye."

"Better not let her hear you calling her that. She'll slap you with a defamation of character lawsuit." Eileen looked at her next card. Grace had been all of ten when she'd announced she was too grown up to be called Gracie, and heaven help the brother who forgot. She might have been the youngest and a girl, but *damn* she could keep those boys in line.

The memory of her family young and carefree and cute and occasionally brawling made Eileen grin from deep down. She missed those days, more than she ever would have imagined when she'd come to help her sister with Grace, and their entire world had shifted off its axis and plummeted into another dimension.

The original plan had been to stay on while Sean found the right housekeeper. Of course, no one had seemed good enough to Eileen, and sooner than she thought, she'd found herself thinking like her sister and playing mama. And she was okay with that. Singing was something she'd always loved. But not anywhere near as much as these kids.

"Eileen? You in?" Dorothy stared at her.

"Oh. Yes." She had no idea what cards were in her hand, but she tossed a chip into the pot, quickly shuffled her cards around and discarded the most useless. "Three."

"Well, I think it would be nice if Grace stayed in town."

So did Eileen, but she'd given up on talking her niece out of conquering the world. Hadn't she felt the same way at that age? "Not happening." At least not yet.

Sally May shrugged. "You never know. Twelve months ago, I would have bet all the cows in Texas not one of the Farradays would be married by the end of the year."

"And not just one but three down and three on deck." Dorothy shook her head and tossed her cards down. "I'm out."

"Would be nice to marry Grace off too." Ruth Ann tossed in a chip. "All the cousins would start popping out around the same time."

"We are talking about Grace Farraday?" Sally May almost choked on her iced tea. "The same Grace who babysat for the Rankin's youngest and parked her in the high chair in front of the fish tank for two hours so Grace could watch *A Few Good Men* uninterrupted?"

Nodding, Dorothy pulled her cards to her breast. "And charged sales tax at the lemonade stand *with* a premium surcharge if folks wanted a maraschino cherry?"

Ruth Ann chuckled. "Okay. Okay. I give. What was I thinking? Our Grace is going to be the country's first female former CEO to be elected president."

All the heads at the table bobbed.

Smiling, Sally May laid down her cards. "Two pair. Queens and tens. Besides, the dog hasn't shown up yet."

"Oh, Lord. Don't tell me she's got you waiting for the dog too?"

Sally May shrugged. "You have to admit, no one else in town has seen the dog except the single Farradays."

Ruth Ann laid down a pair of aces and leaned back in her seat, shaking her head at another lost hand. "And their future wives."

"You too?" Dorothy's eyes widened at her friend. "You're all nuts."

"Well, considering one of the people to see the dog was your granddaughter, soon to be Rebecca Farraday." Ruth Ann shrugged. "You should be a believer too."

"There is no way anyone is convincing me that a stray dog is playing matchmaker."

Eileen was not wasting her breath on this argument. That dog, stray, wild, whatever you want to call it, had picked the perfect match for her boys and she wasn't getting on any marital bandwagon for Grace without that animal's blessing. Period.

"Well," Dorothy folded her cards and set them face down, "I've got bupkis."

Over Dorothy's shoulder, Eileen caught a glimpse of a movement low to the ground coming toward her. Lifting her gaze to focus out the window, she saw Gray trotting up the street from the direction of the feed store. An overwhelming urge to grin as wide as the Red River struck her. Glancing down at her cards, she realized she held a full house. Kings and Aces.

Smiling like a fool, Eileen set her cards down. "Looks like I'm going to win."

• • • •

Only two things were possible. Insanity ran in the Farraday family or the rancher had a damn strange sense of humor. Either way, nothing in all of Chase's diverse background had trained him for how to respond to such a blatant…what? Set up?

Grace shook her head. A very pretty head. "Ignore these two buffoons. They've been hit in the head too many times." Turning an icy glare on them, she slowly enunciated. "By me."

Despite the ludicrous pronouncement, Chase found himself grinning too. The sister had a bit of a temper and something about it struck him as entertaining.

"What are you laughing at?" The icy glare turned on him.

Snapping his mouth shut, he swallowed his smile and stuck out his hand. "Nothing. Nice to meet you."

For a few seconds she stared at his hand as though it were a trap, or perhaps would merely give her the bubonic plague, before blowing out a sigh and accepting it. "Welcome to Tuckers Bluff."

He nodded. "And I am sorry about the dog. Are you okay?" It was a stupid question, considering she looked perfectly fine. Better than fine. But he was willing to bet his latest investment that anything else he could say would only get him into trouble.

"Yes. Thank you." Straightening her shoulders, she spun to face her brothers, a graceful turn proving the hard landing had not been the action of a klutz. "The social club is calling it an early day. I tried calling you to let you know I'm going to stay for dinner tonight at Becky's with Joanna. Aunt Eileen is going to need a ride back to the ranch."

Frowning, Finn slid his cell out of his pocket, tapped at the phone and pressed the side. "Damn phone is acting crazy. The ringer is turned off."

"That can be a sign your battery is on its last leg," Chase offered, taking a step toward Grace and setting the upended display on its feet again. "You may want to replace it sooner than later."

Finn nodded. "Will do. I have to stop in at Sisters to check on something Joanna ordered." He turned to Grace. "I'll be a little bit longer. Want to wait for a ride to the café?"

"I haven't lived in the city that long. I can walk up the street."

"I can give you a lift," DJ offered, leaning over and picking up a few packets of seeds by his feet.

"Thanks, but I really can walk."

DJ handed off the seed packages to Chase. "Then I'd best get moving. Told Esther I'd only be a minute." He followed his brother out the door, leaving their sister standing in front of Chase with seed packets in each hand.

"Thanks." Chase accepted the fallen items and stuffed them quickly onto the display.

"You should sort them. No one likes grabbing a stack of marigolds only to find a rogue flower."

"Yeah, well, I'll reorganize later."

She yanked the seeds out of his hand. "It's easier to do as you go. Why stack the shelves twice?"

He glanced at the Point of Sale display and back at her. The woman had a point. The way she sorted, stacked, and shifted, he had the distinct feeling she'd done this before. Having scooped up the last of the stray packets strewn across the floor, Chase handed her one and stepped back. Not only had she helped fill the shelves, she'd readjusted the placement of the entire display. Not much. Just a few inches and the angle, but it worked better, was still in plain sight but not in the way. "Looks good."

Brushing her hands together, Grace nodded with satisfaction and glanced at the stack of ropes he'd piled on the opposite wall. "What are you doing with those?"

"They were too disorganized. I'm going to hang them back on the wall in better sequence."

Brows arching nicely over pretty blue eyes, dipped together. "Better how?"

"Color for one thing."

"Color?" Her brows lifted high on her forehead and for a split-second Chase was convinced he read awe in her gaze, and not in a good way.

"Is there a problem with sorting by color?"

"That works great for a filing system, but no so much for cattle ropes."

Curious, Chase crossed his arms. "Oh, why is that?"

She pointed at the green rope on top. "That's a head rope." Her finger lowered pointing to another rope underneath in a similar shade. "That's a heel rope."

Head? Heel? The single day old man Thomas had actually shown up to give Chase the promised hands-on training, the guy hadn't said a word about head or heel ropes.

"The orange ones are ranch ropes," she added. "Those you could sort by length. Mr. Thomas stocks mostly 50 or 100 foot lengths."

At least sorting the orange by color worked. He debated how foolish he wanted to look asking questions and decided if color-coding wouldn't work for rope, he couldn't look any more incompetent. "I'm going to take a risk here and assume head rope is for a cow's head and heel rope for their feet?"

Grace nodded. "Head rope is also softer and shorter. Heel rope for the hind legs is sturdier and three feet longer. Though some ranchers use it working cattle, it's mostly for rodeo events and the like."

He'd ask what *the like* was another time. "So put it back the way it was?"

With a shrug, Grace held her hands out, palms up. "Most ranchers place orders for pick up, but if someone does come in and shop, they're probably used to head ropes to the left and heel ropes to the right."

It made sense. When he'd stepped out on a limb and bought this place, Chase knew there'd be a learning curve. But he'd expected more of a helping hand from the former owner, especially with the owner financing agreement they'd made.

"Where's Andy?" Grace looked past the open doorway to the storage and office areas.

"Andy?"

"The clerk?"

Chase shook his head. "I was told Mr. Thomas' son and his wife ran this place on their own."

Those active eyebrows shot up again. "Really?"

"Not true?"

"Mr. Thomas' son hasn't been running the store for quite a few months. Andy is the funeral director, but he would work here part time when business was slow. Marge, the other full time clerk, left when Jake the younger took over. Though that might explain why they had such a hard time of it. When things get busy it can be overwhelming for only two people."

"And you know all this how?"

That brow arched again. "This is a small town. If you have any secrets, you'd better bury them deeper or reveal them now because it won't take long for the whole town to know what time your alarm goes off and the expiration date on that carton of milk in your fridge."

Where everyone else in town he'd had the pleasure to visit with had warned him of pretty much the same thing, the earlier notices had come with a loving hint of pride in their community. Grace's words had come out with the disdain of a teen caught necking in a car by the town gossip. "I don't have any secrets." *Not really.*

"Bully for you." Grace ran her hands down her jeans, and shook her head. "Sorry. I'm not being very gracious."

"Considering you took a dive in my store due to my failure to restrain a stray animal, I'd say not suing me is gracious enough." A hint of a smile crossed her lips and Chase found himself wishing he could see her face light up with laughter.

"I've been away from home for a lot of years now."

Chase considered that. A lawyer, her brothers had warned him.

"Keeping up with the comings and goings of folks doesn't take much more than a Sunday supper, but in all fairness," she teased him with a little more smile, "in high school I worked here part time."

"I see."

"But I should warn you, any rancher will tell you the difference between a head rope and a heel rope and it will have nothing to do with colors." This time a full-fledged grin bloomed and Chase decided small town living definitely had a great deal to offer.

• • • •

"Tell me something." Grace shifted her weight and studied the handsome man in front of her. The short hair, polo shirt, khakis, even with the fresh-out-of-the-box-shiny cowboy boots, screamed big city businessman. "Why a feed store?"

Dang, this character had one hell of a nice smile. He'd done it more than once and Grace wasn't liking the fuzzy feelings bouncing around inside her. The first guy in a hell of a long time to make her feel all girly, and it had to be a delusional businessman planting roots in West Texas.

"Why not?"

"It doesn't take an FBI profiler to figure out you know nothing about farming, ranching, or life in general in rural West Texas."

"I'm a fast learner."

Ignoring the evasive answer, she took a second to glance around the old feed store. Rearranging the ropes hadn't been the new owner's only effort. Fresh displays had been set up in key places, including the flower seeds she'd sent flying. "What's going over there?" She pointed to an empty end cap at what used to be the joint and vitamins aisle.

"New halter and lead rope stock coming in." He crossed his arms. "Nylon." The corners of his mouth tipped north. "Colorful."

Maybe the guy wasn't as daft as she thought. For years folks had wanted old man Thomas to expand his line from the standard rancher leather and boring brown. She herself had ordered tack online in different colors for different horses. "Have you ever even been to a ranch? A working ranch," she added quickly, in case the guy had done a hayride at a party ranch.

"Not many ranches in suburban New York City."

Grace tried not to wince as visions of the city slickers on horseback from every western comedy since her childhood flashed through her mind. "I'm surprised my aunt hasn't already invited you out to the ranch yet, but we'd be pleased to show you around if you join us for supper on Sunday."

Mr. City Slicker's eyes creased with deep-set laugh lines. "Thank you, but you're right, your aunt is expecting me for dinner tomorrow."

"Good." Shoving the offer to stay and help with the ropes out of the way, she nodded and took a step toward the front door. "Call Andy. He's always needed a little extra work between...clients. If you haven't cleaned out the desk already, the phone numbers are taped to the top of the pullout shelf on the old oak desk in the main office."

Chase nodded. "I'll take a look. Thank you."

She could see the windmills of his mind spinning and churning. Probably calculating how to afford extra help. Poor guy was probably going to lose his shirt on this deal. Even if her brothers could show him around the ranch, no way the city slicker could pick up on the needs of a working cattle ranch fast enough to make a go of the feed store. Too bad. She liked his smile.

CHAPTER THREE

"Maybe we should have eloped." Becky blew out a sigh and scrubbed at her face with so much vigor Grace could feel her childhood friend's frustration. "The dress was supposed to be here last week."

"And they promised it would be at the boutique on Monday." Grace spoke especially softly in an effort to add a bit of calm to the conversation.

"I should have just bought one of the samples off the rack."

"And you would have looked lovely, but you looked amazing in the dress that's arriving on Monday."

Becky leaned back and grinned. "I did, didn't I?"

"DJ is going to swallow his tongue when he sees you coming down the aisle."

"I've been around long enough to know," Joanna handed the bride-to-be a glass of wine, "DJ would swallow his tongue if you came down the aisle in a potato sack. The guy is totally over the moon for you."

Grace accepted the glass Joanna handed her. There was a lot of that lovesick gazing going on at the ranch. Every time Grace turned around it was like she'd fallen into a book of fairytales. Each one with a beautiful princess and her handsome prince.

Becky took a slow sip of wine and blew out an equally long slow breath. "I could say the same about Finn."

"I hope so." Joanna lifted her glass to Becky and, grinning like a besotted teen invited to the prom by the captain of the football team, took a sip of her wine. "This stuff is really good. Where'd you get this?"

"Local winery." Grace set her glass on the table.

"Here?" Joanna swallowed hard.

"We're in the high plains. Apparently it's good for growing grapes. One of the Bradys started the vineyard five or six years ago. Things are finally starting to come around for them."

"West Texas is just full of surprises." Joanna leaned back. "So, the plan is we all drive to Dallas Monday if the dress doesn't come?"

"It will come. I think I put the fear of God and the Supreme Court into her if it's not." Grace shrugged. "Besides, I checked the tracking information and it should be crossing the Texas border any minute now."

"For someone who doesn't want to actually practice law," Becky kicked her shoes off, "you sure do threaten to sue a lot of people."

"I thought you were home for the wedding and to study for the bar exam?" Joanna asked.

"I am."

"But you're not planning on practicing law?"

"That's right." Grace held her arm up, looking at the pretty coating on the inside of the glass. Most people thought her nuts for going to law school without a plan for practicing law, but most folks didn't know that a good MBA program cost about the same as her law degree and she'd bypassed MBA and gone straight to the Doctoral pay level. "If I don't take the exam all future employers will think I'm stupid or failed or some combination of both."

"And studying in earnest begins the day after my wedding." Becky grinned at her friend, the few sips of wine she'd had already mellowing her out. She always was a lightweight. "Shall we go over the checklist?"

"Sweetie," Grace set her glass on the coffee table and leaned forward, "nothing has changed since girls' night last night. There are enough people working on this wedding to form the best wedding planning company west of the Mississippi. Relax and enjoy the movie."

There was a time when Grace wanted what Becky had—a good man, a good job, and comfortable shoes. They'd planned their weddings and dreamed up their pretend princes. By the time high school had come and gone, Becky was deep in the dream of white picket fences and two point five children with a litter of puppies. Grace, though, had grown restless, watching her brothers leave the ranch one by one. She'd soaked in all the stories of places far away, things beside ranching, and life in the fast lane. Life had more to offer than West Texas, and her newly bestowed degrees were going to make sure she got to enjoy every minute.

• • • •

Rolling his neck from side to side, Chase stretched his arms, then slammed the lid shut on his laptop. "I can't thank you enough for all the help."

"Considering your background doesn't have a lick of merchandising or animal sciences, you've got a pretty good handle on the situation."

Chase shrugged. "Some merchandising." Marketing, merchandising, advertising, microeconomics, macroeconomics, statistics and a laundry list of other business classes had floated around ungrounded in his head for years. It was more fun than he'd expected pulling tidbits of information from the files of his mind and giving them real life application. "But even the best of MBAs doesn't prepare a person for evaluating the differences in equine joint meds or vitamins for cattle."

Smiling, Adam scratched at his head. "Yeah, I'm going to guess fly repellant wasn't a top priority in business school either."

"No," Chase chuckled, "I may have skipped that session."

"You gentlemen done talking veterinary medicine?" Meg carried a wooden tray and set it on the massive table in front of her husband and Chase.

Chase sniffed at the air. "Man, that smells good."

"That's because it is." Adam smiled up at Meg and scooted over so she could sit beside him on the comfortable sofa.

Meg gently patted her husband's knee. "It doesn't hurt that I'm not the one who baked it."

"There is that," Adam teased, stabbing the warm cinnamon cake with a fork.

"Does it help that I sprinkled the cinnamon on top of the icing?" Meg offered her husband a toothy grin.

"Absolutely," Chase muttered through a mouthful. "Sorry," he swallowed, "this really is fantastic." He was seriously going to have to order gym equipment if he stayed on here much longer.

"Was my husband able to help you?"

"Definitely." Chase took a sip of the coffee. "I could tell by the expiration dates that the previous owner was overstocked, but getting a handle on when and where Mr. Thomas lost control of supply and demand has been more challenging than I'd hoped. I've chatted with some of the ranchers as orders have come in, but I needed more of a crash course."

"Visiting the ranch tomorrow should help too." Adam stabbed at his own cake.

"It was very nice of your aunt to invite me over."

Adam shrugged. "I'd think by now most of the folks would have given an invite of some kind."

"I'm not sure how many most is, but I've taken rain checks with the sisters. By the way," Chase set down his fork, "what are their names?"

Laughter rumbled from deep in Adam's chest.

"I know!" Meg waved her hands high. "It's crazy."

"I think most of us didn't realize we didn't know their Christian names until folks new to town started asking. It seemed perfectly normal to be Sister and Sissy."

Normal? Okay. He supposed, if he and his father never questioned why Deputy Barney Fife didn't have a gun and Otis always slept off his drunk in an unlocked cell, Chase could accept

Sister and Sissy without question. "I've also passed on an invite to the Rankin's and the Bradys."

"Which Brady?"

"There's more than one rancher named Brady?"

Meg nodded. "There's a slew of them. Big ranching family way back but now they're divvied up in different things."

"Got it. The invitation came from Sam."

"Yep. He has the biggest of the Brady spreads. The younger folks have less land, but most of them aren't into ranching anymore."

"So why did you take a rain check on all the others and not Aunt Eileen's?"

"I'm pretty sure I tried, but by the time I got off the phone, I was committed to following Mr. Farraday after church."

"She did it to me too," Meg chuckled. "Amazing gift of...persuasion."

Chase shrugged. "I'm glad. I've been burying my head in cleaning out the old stock, learning the customers, bringing the store up to the new millennium, and not coming up for air."

"Sounds like you can take the boy out of the city, but you can't take the city out of the boy." Meg took a sip from the teacup she held in two hands.

"Works the other way around too." Adam squeezed his wife's knee and nodded at Chase. "Can't be easy giving up the pace of life in New York City for our little town."

From where Chase sat, he could see a hint of more serious thoughts tumbling around behind the smiling eyes. "New York is a different world in so many ways."

"Damn fun too." Meg set her cup on the saucer. "In college we'd take the train down to the city, see a show with the half-price tickets, eat a hot dog from a street vendor, or in winter walk Fifth Avenue looking at all the store windows and eating warm chestnuts."

Adam smiled. "Ah, the famed chestnuts roasting on an open fire."

"Yep. So good." The way Meg ran her tongue across her lips was almost enough to make Chase put a trip home this winter on his to-do list.

Some of the best parts of where he grew up were the things the tourists did. Having access to Broadway shows, the skating rink at Rockefeller Center, or the Circle Line on the Hudson any day of the week if the spirit moved you was a definite perk. Of course the problem for most locals wasn't access but time. Hard to ride up the river and eat a lobster roll, or enjoy center orchestra seating, when the work week is eighty hours long for six or seven days a week.

When he'd finally come up for air it wasn't live theater, or roasting chestnuts, or ferry boat rides he craved. Chase was not going to work himself to death in a concrete jungle. He would enjoy homemade pie, slow walks down an empty street, friendly neighbors, town gossips, and Sundays where family dinners mattered more than the bottom line. No matter how long it took or how much it cost him, he was going to make his new life in Tuckers Bluff work or die trying.

CHAPTER FOUR

"How's that hand holding up?" Sean Farraday stood at the hood of his massive pickup truck, an amused twinkle in his eyes.

Flexing the fingers of his right hand as he approached the family patriarch, Chase couldn't help but smile back. Today had been his first visit to the white clapboard country church and he'd shook hands with more people than a bridegroom in a receiving line. "I may have to start lifting weights or something."

Sean tipped his head back and laughed. "Gotta watch out for Mabel Berkner. She's got one helluva grip."

Shaking his hand, Chase nodded. "That would have to be short, big smile, bright floral dress, and tall, skinny dude at her side."

"That's the one." Still grinning, Sean escorted him inside.

Driving under the scrolling F, behind the parade of trucks and SUVs making their way home for the weekly Sunday supper, Chase had come close to letting go of the wheel and pinching himself. Surrounded by bubbly and friendly people in a town the size of a postage stamp compared to Manhattan, he could almost convince himself he lived in any small town anywhere in the United States. Maybe even Mayberry. But out here there was no denying he was definitely in Texas.

The matriarch, Aunt Eileen, had been the first to leap out of a truck and hurry into the house. Big hats and bustling people flowed from the cars and into the house. A few women carried covered dishes. Like a good host, Sean had waited for Chase before going inside. He might just pinch himself anyway.

"You look a little shell shocked." Sean chuckled as they crossed the threshold into the large living room. "Take a seat. How about a cool beer to treat what ails you?"

Chase nodded. "That would hit the spot."

"Beer coming up," a deep voice called from the kitchen.

He spotted one of the brothers in a nearby doorway, swinging an arm back then forward. Chase prepared to catch a launched bottle.

"Connor, don't you dare," sounded loud and clear from the kitchen.

The guy let out a howling laugh and walked up to Chase. "Teasing my aunt is always so much fun."

"You'd better watch it." Sean shook his head. "One of these days she might tan your hide. Again."

The fatherly threat only made the younger man smile even wider. "Sorry I haven't had time to come into town and say a proper hello. Things at my place have been going a little crazy."

Chase ran through his study session last night with Adam and his wife. Connor would be the one with the horse ranch at the property next door. "No apologies necessary."

"Aunt Eileen has you scheduled out."

"Excuse me?"

"You're going to do the ranch tour before supper and then after dessert, I'm to take you over and show you my operation."

A low chuckle escaped before he could stop himself.

"Did I miss something?" Sean cast a perplexed glance from one man to the other.

Shaking his head, Chase smiled. "If anyone had told me a year ago I would have gotten a jolt of excitement at the prospect of checking out a horse ranch, I would have driven them straight to Bellevue Mental hospital for evaluation."

Connor tipped his beer bottle at him. "Wait. The smell of horses and fresh hay gets in your blood."

"Just don't step in any manure." Grace circled the sofa and sat beside her brother. "I've been sent by Aunt Eileen to make sure you don't fill his mind with useless malarkey."

Connor's eyebrows inched up at his sister.

"Hey," she raised a hand, palm open, "complain to the woman in charge. Those are her words, not mine."

A pretty, light-haired brunette walked in and sat in the chair opposite Chase. "Apparently until I'm officially a Farraday, I'm not allowed in the kitchen." If he remembered correctly, this woman was engaged to the youngest brother.

"That makes two of us." Another attractive young woman, this one with long blonde hair, sat in the other chair.

If Chase was going to start guessing, he'd say the blonde had lived in this part of the country longer. Her boots were clean but well broken in and her church clothes looked more like afternoon picnic attire, while the first woman had on comfortable loafers and leaned toward business casual. Grace, on the other hand, was an interesting blend. She wore boots, but they didn't look like anything she'd be mucking stalls in. Rather than a skirt and blouse, she sported a tan dress with just a pop of country color. Definitely country chic.

"I've been kicked out too." DJ came in and pulled a nearby chair up next to the pretty blonde. Yep. The hometown girl who captured the wrong brother's heart. Meg had told him the story on one of his first nights in town.

One by one the men made their way into the room. Chase listened eagerly as the conversation shifted from pasture rotation, to horses throwing a shoe, to progress on the new fences, to updates on DJ and Becky's wedding in less than two weeks.

"You'll come of course," Becky beamed.

"I'd be honored." From what he'd gleaned of the plans, DJ and Becky were to have a huge blowout celebration and it sounded like not only the entire town was on the guest list, but possibly the whole county.

Chatter picked up again. One of Finn's bulls had to be separated from the herd. If Chase understood correctly, the animal tried to breed a cow across a fence and actually broke his pecker. Who knew?

DJ pushed to his feet and pointed at Chase's empty bottle. "Another beer?"

"No, thanks. One is more than enough at this time of day."

"In that case, ready for a tour?" Connor stood.

"Absolutely." Eager for a better perspective, Chase was on his feet and following Connor in a flash.

"We'll start in the house, then Finn will take you around the barn. You ever been on a horse?"

"A real one?"

Connor laughed and shook his head as he walked across the foyer. "I'll take that as a no. Let me show you the study and what were the original parts of the house, then I'll pass you off. I don't know that Finn's going to want to put you on a horse today. Aunt Eileen has a lot for us to show you."

Following on Connor's heels, Chase nodded and listened as his host explained in great detail how his several times great grandfather had built the smaller original house for his new bride and how through the generations the house had been added onto until very little resembled the old Farraday homestead.

"Ours is one of the few ranches in this part that still has some original structure. Most of the ranches just built new nearby and eventually let the old homesteads succumb to Mother Nature." Doubling back around, Connor stopped in a doorway just off the foyer. "This is my father's haven. Though Finn uses it as much, if not more, now."

Chase stepped into the large room splattered with comfortable leather furniture, book-filled sturdy wood shelving to one side, and a massive oak partner's desk tucked in the only corner of the room to reflect modern technology. "Except for the computer in the middle of the desk, the rest of the room reminds me more of a gentleman's club than an office."

"In many ways it is. Grace and Aunt Eileen have free reign, but it was us boys who spent time in here with Dad. Whether talking cattle and ranching, woman trouble, or merely seeking solace from the madness of the outside world."

A simple nod of the head conveyed his understanding. Not that Chase knew exactly what Connor referred to, but he did have a pretty damn good idea how cruel the world could be. Though he was pretty sure the dark curtain that had drawn on Connor's eyes had little to do with the cutthroat business world, and everything to do with things Chase could only reluctantly imagine. Turning to exit, he spotted the glass-covered shelves on the opposite side of the wall—shelf after shelf of trophies and belt buckles the size of hubcaps. Without thinking to ask, he edged over and took a look. Everything had something to do with horses or rodeos.

Connor appeared at his side. "Most of those seem a lifetime ago."

His gaze went from one shelf to another. The majority seemed to be for barrel racing. "This is a world away from my friends and me. For me, captain of the hockey team was a big deal. But this. I'm not sure which is more frightening, facing a wall of two hundred pound linemen or one pissed-off bull."

"The bull," Connor chuckled.

Chase spun about and looked at the relaxed way Connor leaned against one of the cabinets, arms crossed, a knowing grin on his face. "You were captain of the football team?"

"Only after Brooks graduated."

"I should have known." He returned his gaze to the trophies. "Who was the barrel racer?"

"That would be Grace."

"Holy…" That was not what he'd expected. Something in his city-born-and-bred brain didn't compute a lawyer with a rodeo championship. More than one.

"There's a lot more to my sister than meets the eye." Connor opened another cabinet door and pulled out a similar trophy. "She came by it honestly."

This one had some weight to it, the silver toned silhouette most likely made of real metal. Almost thirty years ago.

"Our mother. One and only time she ever competed. Did it to surprise Dad." He replaced the trophy in its proper place. "Shocked the hell out of him was more like it. Dad said she was a natural. Easily could have been world champ. Of course he did give some credit to the horse." The guy chuckled again. "But even the best of horses needs a rider who can almost become one with their ride."

"I bet." Chase didn't have to be a championship horseman to get that. He'd actually watched a bunch of rodeo shows on TV once he got the harebrained idea to follow up on the ad. Watching the rider corner the barrels and then fly out of the arena had been a favorite event. His mind tried to picture the attractive woman in the other room on a horse racing around the barrels. The image simply didn't register. On the other hand, he was having an equally hard time envisioning the boot-clad woman in a city courthouse. Connor had certainly gotten one thing right. There had to be more to Grace Farraday than met the eye.

• • • •

"Sweetie, go see if the men have fallen down a drain pipe." Aunt Eileen leaned to her left, glancing down the main hall. "I'd like Chase to get a chance to look around outside as long as he wants before supper time."

"Sure." Not that she'd admit it out loud, but Grace was wondering why the brief tour was taking so long. At the foot of the hall, she could make out the male voices coming from her dad's office. As a little girl she'd loved curling up on the big leather chair to do her homework while her father pored over the record keeping. Everything was so simple then. Hand on the doorjamb, she spun into the room the same way she would have when she was only eight years old and eager to spend an evening with her father.

The sight of the two men at the trophy cabinets drew her to a sudden stop. It was bad enough that her father insisted on keeping those blasted trophies on display. Chase was eyeing the oldest one and a familiar pang pinched in her chest. All grown up and moved away, and she still missed her mother. From the time she was first old enough to truly understand Aunt Eileen wasn't her mother, and no matter how many stories or pictures she listened to or stared at, it hurt knowing she'd never have memories of her own to keep alive.

Connor returned the award to its proper place and Grace swallowed hard, her feet unexpectedly heavy. Plastering on the same happy grin she had every time anyone in the family pulled that favored memory of their mother, she threw her shoulders back and sailed into the room. "Whatever my brother has said, don't believe a word."

Their handsome visitor turned his attention to her. "All right."

"That was too easy." Grace came to a stop beside her brother. "Did he tell you about the bull who threw him in Abilene after only two seconds and spent the next five minutes chasing him around the clown can?"

Chase shook his head.

"Then Connor didn't mention when he thought is was a great idea to try to bulldog the neighbor's longhorn, not realizing that the horns were just a little too long to flip and he ended up with a butt full of cactus for Aunt Eileen to pick out."

Another shake.

"He's here to learn about ranching and the supplies we need," Connor rolled his eyes at his little sister, "not about the rare misstep any of us may have taken."

"Misstep huh?" She adored teasing her perfect brothers. Connor and Brooks were the best targets. Adam and Finn let her efforts roll off like water on a duck, but DJ and Ethan fired back as good as they got.

"Did you pop by just for this walk down memory lane?"

"Aunt Eileen wants Chase to have time to hit the barns."

"Right." Chase stepped back from the cases.

"Knock-knock." Connor's wife appeared in the doorway. "Sorry to interrupt. Stacey has a tummy ache and I want to get her home before she shares."

"How bad a tummy ache?" Immediately, Connor crossed the room to his wife. Grace loved watching her brothers as daddies. At times it was harder to process than others, but overall she adored seeing them so happy. Not that they'd ever been unhappy, at least not that she knew. But this was something surreal. She didn't quite get it, but if all went as she hoped, soon she'd be far away and happy as the proverbial clam.

CHAPTER FIVE

Stepping into the living room, the complete shift in mood was palpable. Where everyone had been friendly and playful mere minutes ago, the movement in the kitchen had slowed, and the family sat in silence. Chase didn't have to be an expert on family relations to know something considerably more serious than a grandchild with a possible stomach virus was going on.

Immediately DJ jumped up from his seat and bolted toward his sister. The tight press of his lips and sliver of sorrow in his eyes confirmed Chase's assumption. Something big had happened. He dared a glance at Grace, inching up at his side. Standing stiffly beside him, the tension in her shoulders and the wideness in her gaze reflected the apprehension building inside Chase. He had no reason to be affected by whatever news was coming, and yet, already his heart ached for Grace.

"Sis." DJ's voice came out low and strained.

Grace's hand shot to her right and grabbed onto Chase's. Instinctively his fingers curled with hers and he squeezed. He had no idea what was about to go down, but at this moment he felt as responsible for her as her brothers looming around the room. Her hand held so tightly onto his, he'd have sworn on the Bible he could feel the pounding of her pulse.

"What happened?" Her gaze shifted around the room. "Is it Ethan?" Her eyes flew open even wider, fear and concern replaced with horror. "Not Brittany?"

"No." DJ reached out, gently laying a hand on her shoulder. "It's Dale."

Grace swallowed hard and Chase wondered if she too was engaged and somehow that was the one tidbit none of the locals had clued him in on.

"There's been an accident—"

"He cancelled dinner last month. Said it had been a difficult week." Grace still hung on to Chase's hand despite the nearness of her brother.

DJ nodded. "He was the first responder on a domestic disturbance call a couple of months ago. The family was dead before he even arrived. Not a thing he could have done differently. I tried to talk him into taking some vacation time. Coming to the ranch."

"I don't understand. What does that have to do with the accident?"

Running his hand heavily across the back of his neck, DJ blew out a heavy sigh. "Sometimes it's hard to forget. Memories come whether you want them to or not."

"What happened?" Her voice grew stronger, almost angry.

"Single car accident. He was driving too fast. His blood alcohol level was—"

"Is he—?"

"ICU. Stable. The next forty-eight hours will tell." DJ shook his head. "His mother called me. He's surrounded by family."

Tears welled in her eyes. "Good. Good. He shouldn't be alone." Some of the color returned to her cheeks.

To Chase, the grip on his hand eased away in what felt oddly like slow motion. Blinking, Grace lifted her chin, muttered "*damn war,*" and walked out of the room, pausing in his line of sight to the kitchen to kiss her aunt on the cheek, and continued walking away. An overwhelming need to follow her and somehow wash away her pain pulsed forcefully through his veins, but none of this was any of his business.

"One of us should go after her," Adam said, his gaze shifting to the others in the room.

The younger brother Finn shook his head. "She's off to see Princess. Give her a few minutes."

Brooks and their father nodded and Adam turned to DJ. "What about you, man? You okay?"

"I will be." DJ's fiancée sidled up beside him, her hand about his waist. "I knew he was having a hard time. The tone of his voice. Nothing specific he said, more what he didn't say."

"Maybe you should go?" Concern shone in Becky's gaze.

DJ shook his head. "I'd only be in the way. His family is what he needs."

"Are you sure?" Becky leaned against him.

"Yeah." DJ nodded. "Yeah, I am."

"I should..." Chase looked at the solemn faces and remembered the tears in Grace's eyes. "Take a rain check, head back to the—"

"No." Sean Farraday pushed to his feet. "In happiness and sadness, family *and* friends are meant to be together."

Beyond any doubt, Chase was not family, but unlike the lip service of big cities, he knew these folks truly did consider him a friend, and with only a few words, he didn't feel like an intruder any more.

The family patriarch turned to the youngest son and nodded.

Finn bobbed his head, and looked to Chase. "Now would be a good time to tour the barn. You up to it?"

"If you are." An hour ago he'd been anxious to see the setup, learn about tack and feed and how the operation ran. Now, he just wanted to make sure a woman he barely knew was okay.

● ● ● ●

"The good guys aren't supposed to lose." Grace pulled another carrot treat out from her pocket for her favorite horse before running her hand down the front of Princess' nose. It made no sense that horses understood people better than humans, but the good ones always did, and Grace couldn't imagine life without the great horses like Princess. Growing up, especially in her teen years, she'd spent many a night out in the barn talking to a horse whose only response was a nudge with its muzzle and a blink from understanding eyes. Hurt feelings and broken hearts always mended more easily after a girls' gab session with Princess. Though she'd need a lot more than a visit to the stable to erase the ache pressing at her chest.

Since Dale's break-up with Grace's roommate Denise, she hadn't seen as much of him, but she missed the late night bull sessions on life, law school and the general immaturity of the male college student. She didn't want to consider he might not make it. The waste of it all had her wanting to kick the oat pail across the barn. Scream at the powers that be who brought a good man back from a damn war and then expected him to carry on as though he'd come home from a ride in the spring countryside.

Perked ears and then one leaning left alerted Grace to the arrival of other people. Princess could hear a mouse in the dog pens before the dogs. She wasn't ready to talk to her family. If anything, they'd think she was overreacting. DJ was the one they should worry about. He and Dale had crossed paths in the Marines and then bonded on the Dallas police department. She should stop throwing a pity party and go check on him. "You be a good girl. I'll come back soon. Promise."

The horse flicked its head up and down, wiggled her lips in what Grace knew was a silent scolding of "you'd better make damn sure" and then poked at her pocket for one last treat.

"Okay." Leaning into Princess' neck, Grace gave another quick hug and pushed away, opening the gate and stepping into the dimly lit center aisle.

"There you are." Finn and Chase were coming at the open doorway to the tack room. "We were just discussing the choices for senior dog food. If he stocked something of a higher caliber than old man Thomas did, maybe more of us would stock up rather than be cooking for the dogs."

Grace nodded. "Good dog is better than a good ranch hand. Wouldn't feed a good ranch hand bread and water."

"Makes sense." Chase glanced to the back of the tack room. Whether he was calculating the costs of readjusting his dog food inventory or taking stock of items he recognized and sold, Grace couldn't tell, but she was positive the man's mind was clicking away and filing data. A smart mind. Though she had to wonder what a smart man was doing setting up business in Tuckers Bluff. A business he clearly knew next to nothing about.

The whizzing sound of a text message filled the small room. Finn pulled his phone from his belt loop, pressed his lips tightly, swiped his finger around the screen then looked up. "Dad's circling the wagons. Wants Connor at supper and he's not answering the phone."

"Do you think it's Stacy?" Grace did not want to think the worst, but life had proven statistics were not always in the Farraday favor.

"I think he's set his phone down somewhere and is either off reading stories to his daughter or making love to his wife."

"I did not need to hear that." Grace rolled her eyes. She didn't care who was married, she didn't want to go anywhere near what her brothers did with their free time. The only thing that made her almost chuckle was the way Chase blinked before looking to Grace and back and smothering a smile. So the city boy had a little southern gentleman in him.

"I'd better run over and check out what's going on." Finn turned to Chase. "You want to come with me or do you want to wait back at the house? Or," he spun about toward Grace, "you want to show him the rest of the area? Remember the things we have to order special?"

"I do and I can." A good distraction would work well for her about now.

Finn looked to Chase. "That good with you?"

"I'm flexible."

Grace moved closer to her brother and the newest member of the community. "Let me know if we're needed inside or if Catherine needs help with Stacey."

"Will do." Finn turned and trotted out the barn.

"Is he going to walk over?"

Shaking her head, Grace dragged her gaze away from Finn and her thoughts away from Connor and DJ. "It's close but not if there's a hurry. He'll probably drive the truck over."

"Got it." Chase looked at the walls of the tack room and back. "I'm sorry about your friend."

She sucked in a long slow breath. "So am I. He's one of the good guys."

"You two were close?" Chase slid his hands into his pockets. "Sorry, it's none of my business."

"That's okay." She leaned against the wall. "We were friends."

He nodded, but she could see what he thought in his eyes.

"Just friends," she explained. "When DJ came back to Tuckers Bluff he asked Dale to keep an eye on me. As if having six brothers wasn't enough. Suddenly I had seven." She chuckled softly. "I only saw him once every few months at first and then he met my roommate Denise."

"They hit it off?" Chase smiled. She liked the way it made his eyes twinkle.

"Like fire and kindling. I got to see quite a bit of him for over a year. After they broke up he still kept his word. We'd have dinner or a drink almost every month, but by then it wasn't such a chore." She shrugged and blinked back the tears. "Don't tell anyone I said so, but it was kind of nice having a seventh brother."

"Maybe you can tell him yourself." Chase stretched out his hand and swiped at the single tear that escaped down her cheek, and then he quickly stepped back, sliding his hands back in his pocket. "When he's feeling better, that is."

"Right." She pushed away from the wall and muttered, "Better."

"Hey." He looked to reach for her again and then, as though thinking better of it, let his hand fall to his side. "Don't give up on him."

She lifted her chin. "I'm not." Even if the odds didn't seem to be in his favor, she had to believe Dale would get through this and snap out of whatever was going on in his head. She tried for a reassuring smile and with a brief nod to cement her decision, she gestured toward the far wall, returning to the job she'd been given. "As you can see, this is the tack room."

In a nod to her efforts, Chase smiled and cast his gaze around the room. "I'm pleased to say I think I know what most of this stuff is." Taking a couple of steps, he picked up a small pair of work gloves. "I don't stock these."

Grace shook her head. "They're for Stacey. She doesn't really spend much time here anymore, but no, Thomas never stocked gloves that small."

Lips pressed tightly, his head bobbed. "And you're not the only rancher who let their young children help out, are you?"

"Family business. We all learn young."

"Including you?"

"Including me. Ranching isn't very sexist."

"No." He put the gloves down with a smile. "So I'm learning."

Leading him down the hall, she returned the grin. "And now you know what a rancher will keep on hand and how much." She moved to another door and pushed it open. "We've got an extra storage area for things we might go through more quickly. Not everyone has enough room for that sort of thing."

Chase nodded. She could see his mind doing mental math again. This guy would be so easy to pick apart in court.

Brows furrowed suddenly, he pointed to the back side of the storage room. The guy had spotted her old colored show harnesses. "Did Thomas special order those?"

"Nope. Ordered 'em online."

"They're yours?" A grin replaced the deep-set concentration of a moment ago.

"They were."

"You don't use them anymore?"

"I don't have time."

His expression shifted in thought again.

"Four years away at college. Three years in Dallas for law school," she answered the unasked question.

"What about summers?"

She shook her head. "In college I worked at the presidential conference center."

Those brows uncurled as his eyes widened with surprise. "Political aspirations?"

"Not a lick, but it looks good on a resume, whether I stuck with law or not."

"And you did."

"Always knew I was going to do law school. Law," she cocked her head, "not so much."

Those brows formed a V again. "Why would you go to law school if you don't want to practice law?"

"Maybe you're not as smart as you look." The cocky grin that spread across his face made her wish she hadn't paid him a complement, even an underhanded one. "I grew up in a small town where a big trip meant going to Houston or Dallas and success always came with the smell of cut hay or manure. When one of the Bradys decided to start a vineyard, the way the town carried on anyone would have thought he'd committed high treason."

"I guess in ranch country a vineyard is a bit of a stretch."

"And isn't that what living is all about? Stretching our limits, our boundaries?"

Chase's head tipped from side to side. "Maybe. And maybe boundaries are just a state of mind?"

"You sound like my dad." Grace led the way toward the larger stalls for birthing and sick animals. "This stall is for our expectant horses or animals that need extra care. And here," she pointed to a few cattle pens, "is where we'll put the expectant cows."

"I thought ranch animals were just born out on the fields."

"Pastures." Grace shrugged. "We separate the expectant cows from the others. At night we put the ones we think are close in the barn. Especially first calf heifers as we may have to help them by pulling their calf."

"Oh." To Chase's credit he hid his flinch well.

Turning back toward the front, Grace paused at Princess' stall to scratch her nose. "I'm all out of treats. You ate them before."

The horse pressed into her hand and Chase came forward. "May I?"

"Sure. Princess is as sweet as they come."

Slowly Chase came at Princess from the side so she'd see him and stroked her down her jawline. "You really are a sweet one. And big."

"She's midsized for a quarter horse. If you want to see big you should see the draft horses. Those suckers could pull the Budweiser wagon."

"No thank you. This is plenty big for me." His attention shifted from Princess to Grace. "I gather she's your horse?"

Grace nodded.

"The one the bright harness was for?"

"That was a long time ago." Sometimes she felt like riding and racing had been the memory of another person's life.

"Yes," he agreed. "I get you've been busy. No time. But do you still ride her?"

Pushing away from the gate, she rubbed Princess one more time. "Not really. We'd better get moving. There's a lot to show you still."

Chase patted the horse the way she had and then followed on her heels. "It's obvious you love your horse. Why don't you ride her anymore?"

"It's not like I haven't gotten on her to help out at some point or other if I'm home. But it's been a while. Like I said, my life isn't wrapped up in this little world anymore."

"Right. Stretching boundaries."

"Exactly."

Stepping ahead of her to slide the barn door open, Chase shrugged. "The grass is always greener."

"This is different."

Chase shrugged. "If you say so."

Didn't she do just that? Soon she'd have DJ's wedding behind her and she could focus all her time on studying for the bar. With a shiny new JD after her name and a passing grade on the bar exam, the world would be hers to enjoy. A world without fences, or livestock, or literal bull shit.

CHAPTER SIX

Any other time and the irony of his and Grace's lives would have given Chase a good laugh. Everything she was running away from was exactly what he'd been dreaming of since the first time his dad and he had sat side by side on the sofa with a big bowl of butter- and cheese-sprinkled popcorn to watch a marathon of the *Andy Griffith Show*.

Only in his case, the grass truly was greener. Or at least yellow. With the exception of Central Park, which he never had time to frequent, concrete made up the better part of the Manhattan landscape.

"Where to now?" he asked.

"I'd better take you back to the house and see what Dad has in mind. If he wants me to walk you through saddling a horse, something else, or wants us all back. Though it makes more sense for you to do it all, saddle, ride, and clean up. Then you'll get a real feel for all the bits and pieces."

"I might have time later this week."

"Oh?" She tilted her head to the side and with one eye closed, looked up at him. Her tone of voice held amused awareness.

He bit back his own smile. "Just before church this morning I had a few minutes to speak with Andy the funeral director."

"Really?" The humor in her voice spread to a broad smile.

"You were right. He's interested in part time work." He shouldn't, but he liked the way her eyes lit up with satisfaction. "We had a nice discussion before we were interrupted. I think he'll be a big help, making it easier for me to maneuver through new territory."

"Keep you from sorting by color?" She didn't even try to muffle the soft chuckle that came with the bright grin.

Man, he liked the way her eyes sparkled when she teased. "Something like that."

"Sounds like a good idea." Approaching the back porch, her footsteps slowed as voices from inside grew louder.

Chase found himself standing a little closer than he normally would, hoping she might reach out and grab his hand again the way she had earlier, even if he strongly suspected she hadn't realized she'd been holding onto him at the time. Coming out of her father's office, the apprehension in her gaze at her brother's approach and the pain that had replaced it from the impact of his words struck Chase surprisingly hard. Since Grace had made no mention of reaching out for him later on, back in the barn, even with no one else but the horses to eavesdrop, he suspected her actions had been driven by sheer shock of the moment. Hell, he'd been as grateful for the human contact and he barely knew this family, and hadn't known the victim at all.

Now, seeing the intensity of her gaze on the back door, he was tempted to offer his hand to steady her steps. Not that they needed steadying. Not now and especially not in a few weeks when she returned to her big-city plans. And there was another reason why he had no business contemplating anything about Grace Farraday. He had a huge task ahead of him. A proving grounds of sorts and he couldn't afford any distractions. Then again, if he'd followed the rules all these years, the last place he'd be is on the back porch of a sprawling cattle ranch daydreaming about holding hands with a pretty girl.

"Everyone seems more animated," Grace added, focusing on the snippets of conversations coming from the house.

He couldn't argue with her there. Grace Farraday was clearly a woman of many talents. Too bad for him those talents weren't planning on making themselves at home in Tuckers Bluff.

The kitchen door opened and the unexpected sounds of dishes clattering, people bustling about, bathed with the occasional chuckle, burst into the open.

Grace's face scrunched with confusion and then her gaze landed across the room. In a flash she bolted inside as though someone had lit firecrackers in her shoes. "Hannah!" The two women collided in a clench worthy of a sappy greeting card commercial.

"What are you doing here?" Grace stepped out of the hug.

"Jamie mentioned he had a few days off and wanted to pop by since he missed the last wedding." Hannah eased back another step. "I had a couple of last minute cancellations so I decided to tag along."

"Well, whatever the reason, I am so glad you're here." Grace turned to face him. "Let me introduce you to the new feed store owner. Chase Prescott, this is my cousin Hannah Farraday."

"Nice to meet you." Chase accepted Hannah's proffered hand. "I gather you guys don't live close."

"Actually," Grace started, but both did a girly giggle he wouldn't have expected from Grace, "we live about thirty minutes apart, but apparently to actually see each other we have to travel halfway across Texas."

"Thirty minutes?" he repeated.

"I rent a condo not far from the law school," Grace provided.

"And I," the other woman joined in, "live in a garage apartment in a suburb on the south end of Dallas. Depending on traffic and time of day I could get to North Dallas in about twenty minutes, or two hours."

"Two hours?" Chase concluded she had to be kidding—even his neck of the woods wasn't that extreme.

"Now, that's an exaggeration," Grace chimed in. "Even in rush hour you can easily get to my condo in…oh…an hour…and a half."

Hannah lifted her left hand onto a hip. "And if there's an accident?"

"I'd see you the next day." Laughing heartily, Grace wrapped an arm around her cousin. "But if you come at two in the morning on a Wednesday night I bet you could make it in twenty minutes."

"Done." Hannah leaned into her cousin. "First Wednesday night you're home you can come visit my place at two a.m."

"Agreed." Grace pulled her cousin into another hug and held on for a little longer than the first embrace, then backed away, looking around. "So, where's that crazy brother of yours?"

Hannah flung a thumb over her shoulder. "He, Adam, Brooks, and DJ are on the front porch with a bottle of Johnny Walker."

"And Dad?" Grace glanced over her cousin's shoulder toward the front of the house.

"He's pouring. Blue label," Hannah added.

Chase had no idea if blue label whiskey was the norm in this part of the country, but even in the circles he moved in, the couple of hundred dollars a bottle blend was not a front porch, Sunday afternoon, shoot the breeze kind of scotch whiskey.

"Come on." Grace slipped her hand through his arm and tugged, hesitated, then stared down at their linked elbows.

The way her cheeks suddenly flushed, he had the distinct feeling she was experiencing a moment of *déjà vu* from about an hour or so ago. "You all right?"

Regaining her composure, she blinked, her gaze locked on his. "Thank you."

"Any time." Beautiful blue eyes seemed to be studying his soul.

With a brief nod, she broke the connection and glanced to the door. "Let's take you to the remainder of your species. I'm sure there's an extra glass awaiting your arrival." Over her shoulder, she looked to Hannah. "Stay put. I'll be right back." A fresh smile on her face, she returned her attention to him. "Ready?"

"As I'll ever be." He might be more than ready for a smooth glass of whiskey, but something deep in his gut told him he might never be ready for everything Grace Farraday had to offer. Not that she was offering, but still, it was hard to ignore the possibilities.

• • • •

"Okay. What was that all about?" Hannah stood halfway between Grace and the kitchen.

Carrying three glasses of lemonade in front of her, Becky came up beside Hannah. "Since the men have the front porch on such a pretty day, the women are moving to the back. And what was *what* all about?"

"Nothing." Grace couldn't answer because she had no idea what the answer would be. When she slipped her arm through Chase's a few minutes ago it was more in jest, but the feel of his arm against hers flashed her back to earlier in the day. It had taken her a few seconds to process if she was actually remembering what had happened or merely undergoing one of those weird psychobabble moments. But the only weird thing was that in a moment of distress she'd reached out for support from a near total stranger. A stranger who had given her much needed strength without comment or question. None of which made any sense to her. She wasn't the sort to need help, never mind to reach out to someone she barely knew, and then not even realize or remember she'd done it. Maybe the pressure of the damn bar exam was more stressful than she was willing to admit. "Nothing at all."

"Well," Becky looked from Grace to Hannah, "if you ask me—"

"I'm not."

"Since when has that stopped me?" Becky just grinned at her long-time friend. "Anything that merits a double nothing is most definitely something. So what happened?"

Hannah looked around and back. "Grace and the new guy were staring at each other as though they could eat each other with a spoon."

"Oh that." Becky shrugged.

"What do you mean oh that?" Grace and Hannah echoed.

"Earlier when DJ had to tell her about Dale, she latched onto Chase as if they'd been a matched set."

"She did?" Hannah looked sideways at her cousin.

"DJ never shows expression," Grace explained. "He's had to deliver sad news to too many people. When I saw the pain in his eyes, I knew it was something bad, but when he said it was Dale…" Tears welled again in Grace's eyes and she had to blink them back more than once. "I hate sad news."

"I knew something was bothering DJ recently," Becky looked to her fiancé on the porch, "but couldn't get him to tell me what. We're still working on him not keeping stuff bottled up. Adam says that strong silent thing is worse for the guys coming back from the military."

Hannah's nod mirrored Grace's. They'd all seen it. Every time DJ or Connor came home from the Middle East they were a little different. Took a little longer to settle in. She was thrilled when they both left the service, Connor sooner than DJ. If the shit Ethan had seen bothered him, he hid it better than his brothers, but Grace wasn't going to lie, she was damn glad they were all out of harm's way now. And as soon as Ethan was finished up in California, all the brothers would be safe at home.

"You've grown awfully quiet." Hannah set her fingers on Grace's arm. "Maybe we should raid the liquor cabinet and spice up the lemonade."

"Said like a true bartender's sister. Jamie would be proud of you."

"Mixologist," Hannah corrected. "We'd better catch up with the ladies out back, and then you can tell us all about the hot new feed store owner."

"You think he's hot?" Grace didn't expect that to bother her.

"You don't?" Hannah's eyes opened wide. "Are you blind, woman? Tall, dark and dreamy fits the bill just right."

Grace resisted turning to take another look herself. Of course she'd noticed he was all of the above. "And delusional. Don't forget that one."

"Huh?" Becky stopped in her tracks. "Where'd that come from?"

"Oh, give me a break." Grace walked past her dear friend and future sister-in-law. "City boy buys a feed store in the middle of nowhere and doesn't even know the difference between a head and heel rope? In my book that's delusional with a capital D."

"I don't care if he's delirious." Hannah fanned under her chin. "Don't find too many of those just hanging around."

"They probably have more just like him in New York." Grace kept moving toward the back. Not that she wanted to continue this conversation with the rest of the female clan, but she didn't want to think more on how hot Chase Prescott was or wasn't. On the other hand, maybe finding herself a New York hottie of her own still living in New York City wasn't a half bad idea at all. The thought made her smile. As soon as she had the bar exam under her belt, a long weekend in New York would be just the reward. After all, her cousin was right about one thing. Who could ignore tall, dark and dreamy?

CHAPTER SEVEN

"**B**est thing about visiting this part of Farraday country is Aunt Eileen's pies." Jamie Farraday, the eldest of Aunt Anne and Uncle Brian's children, flashed the crooked-heart-stealing smile he'd inherited from his father as he dug into the rancher-sized lunch. Grace wondered just how many broken hearts were scattered between Austin and Dallas and anywhere else Jamison Farraday had paused to rest. "Don't tell Mom," Jamie continued, "but no matter how many years she practices, she's just not a baker."

Grace broke open the oven-fresh biscuit, releasing a burst of warm air. Even she missed her aunt's cooking. Despite all the Dallas restaurants boasting world-class biscuits and homemade foods, nothing she'd found so far matched dinner at the family table. "And here I thought you came to see our smiling faces."

"That too, cuz. That too." Jamie chewed and swallowed, and turned to face his cousins. "Have we heard anything new on DJ's friend?"

Several heads shifted from side to side.

"DJ said he'd let us know if there was any change. I'm hoping no news is good news, but I'm going to call the hospital myself shortly. They may not tell me much, but..."

Aunt Eileen poured herself a cup of coffee. "I wish there was something we could do."

Hannah set down her fork. "If DJ's right and his friend Dale was having an emotionally hard time dealing with that domestic violence incident, he's going to need professional help. These military veterans are some of the hardest patients to deal with. They have a tough-it-out-on-their-own attitude. They want to work it off themselves."

"And they can't," Aunt Eileen mumbled. "At least not too many of them."

"Not long ago," Grace interjected, "Dale met someone new. DJ mentioned they'd recently broke it off too. I wonder if that's what set him off?"

"I wouldn't know." Hannah's gaze drifted to the side window and into the distance. "But I wouldn't be surprised if the breakup was a response and not the catalyst. I see it in veterans and cops, a pulling away, distancing themselves from the people they love."

"And Dale was both." Aunt Eileen sat back in her chair.

"Yeah," was all Hannah said before pushing to her feet and taking her dish to the sink.

From where Grace sat at the massive kitchen table, she had a clear view of Connor and Catherine across from her. The two often did that same doe-eyed newlywed eye-gazing thing that all her brothers and their other halves did, but this look was different. There was a silent conversation going on and the undertones were a hell of a lot more serious than two people in love coordinating their next rendezvous. Whatever the silent discussion was about, it ended with Stacey trotting merrily into the room and Connor covering his wife's hand and giving a quick squeeze before pulling his new daughter onto his lap.

"Sorry we're late." Finn hung his hat by the back door. "Thought I was going to have to help with one of our first time mamas."

"Everything okay?" Aunt Eileen was already at the stove dishing out a plateful of stew for the straggling nephew.

"Yeah, mama and son are doing fine."

A wide eyed moment of panic flashed across Catherine's face as she glanced from her young daughter to her brother-in-law. Connor reached over and gently patted his wife's knee and she blew out a soft breath and studied her smiling daughter.

"We gots another calf, mama."

"We have."

Stacey nodded. "We have another calf. This one's all black and wobbly but Uncle Finn let me pet him."

Grace had to give her sister-in-law credit. A few months ago, Catherine would have been hyperventilating at the thought of Stacey that close to a cow and her calf. Now, only a few slow breaths and her husband's hand had her sharing her daughter's joy of discovery.

"Tell them what else we did," Finn encouraged.

Stacey lit up as though she'd been given a first-class ticket to the North Pole. "Uncle Finn let me help feed the 3x4 bales of hay to the cows."

"He did?" Connor said with a hint of exaggeration.

"Yes. He said I was a big help."

Connor pulled her into a tight hug. "I bet you were, partner."

All this sweet family bonding was starting to unnerve Grace. She supposed they did have a relatively functional family life compared to some, especially considering how they lost their mother and all, but all this newfound love and joy and syrup in the room was getting to be a bit much, even for her.

The sound of her cell ringing in the other room startled Grace out of her thoughts. "Excuse me." She popped up from her seat and darted to where she'd left the phone on the end table. "Hello?"

"It's here!" Becky squealed in her ear.

Grace had a pretty good idea what it was, but she asked anyhow. "And that would be the new shipment of antivenom?"

"Sometimes you are too much like your brothers." Becky made an effort at groaning, but her jubilance won out. "My dress. It's at Sisters. Adam said I can take off the rest of the afternoon. Can you meet me?"

Glancing down at her jeans and boots, for a flash of an instant Grace considered heading upstairs to change and put on some makeup, and just as quickly remembered she was in Tuckers Bluff where dressing up meant pressed jeans and taking a brush to your boots. "I'll be there as fast as I can."

"Not too fast," Becky said quickly.

The girl knew Grace a little too well, but how much trouble could she get into on a long lonely stretch of straight road? "I'll pick you up at the clinic."

Becky sounded so excited, Grace wasn't sure the girl was going to be able to wait till Grace got to town.

"I've got to run into town." Grace faced her family, "Becky's dress is here. Okay if I take the white truck?"

"I'm not going anywhere," Finn said. "Take the suburban."

"Got it." Grace smiled at her brother and wondered why none of them had ever bought a nice fast car. She almost laughed when she thought of Ethan. Who needed a car when he could cut through miles of sky at 150 miles per hour.

Rocking to Carrie Underwood and Rascal Flats, Grace made it to town in just over forty-five minutes. Hopefully Becky wasn't paying enough attention to time to notice.

"Oh, you're here," Becky squealed as Grace walked into the lobby. When her gaze lifted up to the clock on the wall, she narrowed her eyes at Grace and shook her head. "Just so you know, if anything had happened to you it would have totally ruined the wedding."

Grace chuckled. "I love you too."

Huddling and laughing like a couple of teenagers trading secrets, they hurried across the street and over to Sisters. The two women must have been as eager as Becky to see the dress as Sister held the door open and Sissy waited a few feet inside with a big white box.

"You can go try it on." Sissy shoved the box at Becky and shooed her toward the dressing rooms.

"Do you want some help, dear?" Sister asked, her gaze hopeful, but Becky's eyes shifted to Grace.

"I'm coming." Grace hurried behind her. In a surreal sort of way this reminded her so much of playing dress up as little girls. When the hell had everyone grown up?

● ● ● ●

"Yes, sir, Mr. Rankin." Andy penned the last item on the order and Chase did his best to look busy behind the counter.

Watching Andy and Mr. Rankin talking brought home how little Chase actually knew about the world he'd bought into. The two discussed the weather and cattle and other things as natural to them as the new restaurant on 8th Avenue or what the closing values of the stock market in China were for him and his associates.

"Sounds like you're feeling right at home?" The middle-aged rancher looked at Chase.

"As a matter of fact, I am." He had to remind himself that one day talking about bailing machines and branding would come as easily to him as it was to the other men in the store.

"Word at the café is that Eileen baked you her blueberry sour cream pie."

"For me?"

"At supper on the ranch," the man clarified.

"Oh. Yes, yes she did."

The bell over the door jingled and another man Chase didn't recognize came in.

"Afternoon Will, Andy," the large man in the standard, jeans, boots, button down shirt and hat extended his hand. "You must be the new owner from New York? I'm Will Berkner."

"Guilty as charged." Chase accepted the man's hand and shook. It hadn't surprised him to hear the customer knew he was from New York; he understood word spread fast when strangers moved to a small town.

For the next few minutes the two customers exchanged chitchat about wives and children and cow tipping. Until that second, Chase had always thought cow tipping to be a joke, not something that teenagers actually did for a prank. Whatever the men spoke of next was lost as Chase pondered how the hell a person gets fifteen hundred pounds or more of cow to lay feet up on its back.

"You still using the Stongid for your horses?" Andy asked.

"I am. Haven't had a lick of trouble with colic or worms since Adam suggested it, but I'm here for a few bales of hay. Been meaning to come into town for almost a week now, but one thing after another. You know how it is."

"That I do," Andy agreed and Stan Rankin nodded.

"What ya think of the Farraday place?" Will asked Chase.

"Nice."

"Nice? They've got one of the most prosperous ranches this side of Fort Worth." Will chuckled. "Burt tells me that with Andy here helping out you'll be able to do some riding with the Farraday boys."

"Burt?" Chase didn't remember mentioning that to anyone but Andy this morning.

"You know," Andy coaxed him, "owns the hardware store."

"Yes, of course."

"If you bring your truck around the back, we'll load that hay for you."

"Sure thing." Will turned to Chase. "Grace and Becky are over at the Sisters picking up the wedding dress."

Chase nodded, not sure if Burt had shared that tidbit as well, or if Mr. Berkner had come by the information some other way.

"She's a nice girl, that Grace. A little wild when she was younger, but nice girl."

"Yes," Chase agreed, careful not to say too much.

"But don't you let the stories of that dog and her brothers push you into asking the girl out. A man's got a right to stay single if he wants."

Chase opted for just nodding again. Was the man making a lucky guess or did he somehow know that the stray wolfdog had flattened Grace out in his store? Surely the man was just talking in generalities.

"Well," the man tapped his hand on the counter, "I'd better get my hay. Nice meeting you and remember what I said about Grace. Don't you let no dog rush you into anything."

"Thanks." Chase raised his hand in a lame effort at a wave.

"I'll walk you out," Stan Rankin said to other man. "I gotta ride around and get my order of horse feed."

As the door closed behind the two men, Chase heard Rankin ask the other one, "Sounds like your money's on city boy. I put ten on the dog."

Rooted in place, Chase stared at the door. Did two people he had never met before really know that much about his life? What was it Grace had said to him? *The whole town will know what time your alarm goes off and the expiration date on that carton of milk in your fridge.* Apparently, she hadn't been kidding. A grin tugged at the corners of his mouth. If folks were going to keep that close tabs on him, he'd have to make sure not to let his milk spoil. Then he was going to have to find out who was running the pool and get in on the bet. He just wasn't sure which side he was rooting for. Yet.

• • • •

"I swear, Dallas won't be far enough away." Grace tossed her keys on Becky's kitchen counter.

"They didn't mean anything by it." Becky hung the bagged wedding dress from the ceiling fan.

Eyeing the dress on display in the center of the room, Grace shook her head. "You're going to hang it there?"

"For now." Her childhood friend grinned. "And it's no big deal that Mrs. Berkner heard Chase and Andy talking about his getting to see more of the ranch one day, and that she told Polly and Polly told Sissy. That's the way things work around here."

"And that's exactly what I mean. Some days I feel like this town knows more about my life than I do." Grace sucked in a deep breath. "Do you really think the town is betting on that dog making another match?"

"I doubt it's the whole town." Becky's attempt at a reassuring smile failed miserably.

"It had to be Burt Larson. That man has eyes on the back of his head."

"Could have been Polly. She's been known to watch the neighbors with binoculars from the Cut and Curl."

"Oh lord." Grace sank onto the sofa. "I seriously don't think Dallas is far enough away. I love the idea that I can get in my car if there's a crisis or blessing and be home in a few hours, but the older I get the more I think an airplane ride of only a few hours isn't such a bad thing."

"You can't possibly mean that?"

"Would it be so awful if I lived some place fun like New York or maybe Boston?"

"I thought you don't like the cold?"

"Okay, then San Francisco or LA."

"Earthquakes and mudslides," Becky deadpanned.

"And Texas is in Tornado Alley. No place is perfect."

"I don't get it." Becky flopped on the chair across from her friend. "You love the horses and the ranch."

"I do, but in moderation. A word that anyone over forty in this town is unfamiliar with."

Shaking her head, Becky leaned heavily back. "It's always nice when you're home for more than a couple of days. I know I'm getting married, but once you start working and only get two weeks of vacation a year, I'm really going to miss you."

"Dallas is only a few hours away."

"Might as well be the moon. Or New York."

Now would probably not be the best time to mention that New York wasn't nearly as farfetched or spontaneous as Grace had made it sound. She'd entertained the idea of a coastal move for months, and when the opportunity arose for a position with one of the country's largest law firms in the Big Apple, Grace hadn't hesitated to send in a resume. Maybe she should have sent a resume to the offices in Paris. She was pretty sure the French Riviera didn't have cold weather, earthquakes, or tornadoes, and what were a few extra hours on a plane ride home?

CHAPTER EIGHT

E xcept for the long drive to the Farradays or any other ranch in the county, Chase could most likely have done without a car. He was also starting to understand why the vehicle of choice in this neck of the woods was either an oversized SUV or one of those ginormous pickups with four doors and enough room to transport an elephant. Or two.

Driving back to the B&B, the diversity of architecture and obvious lack of city planning drew Chase's attention away from the road. Quaint craftsman homes sat beside a few mid-century curiosities and the occasional Victorian. One street in particular seemed to be more heavily lined with the ornate curly cues and tri-color painting of the century-old construction era. The short row of houses reminded him of the famed street in San Francisco used often in commercials and movies. The original ornate homes with the shiny modern city in the backdrop. Where he'd grown up a hundred-year-old house was common, but not so much from the Victorian era. He'd taken a liking to the B&B; owning something like it would be quite the contrast to his modern bachelor apartment in the city. But what the heck would he do rattling around a big old house all by himself?

Maybe it was time to start thinking of a more permanent place to hang his proverbial hat. Staying at Meg and Adam's while he found his footing, or flopped, made sense, but for how long? When would he be sure Tuckers Bluff would be all he'd anticipated? He hadn't really given much thought to how this entire "buy a business and move west" scenario was supposed to play out in the long term, except of course that he would be loved and respected enough as one of the community to overlook his Yankee roots. So far it looked like he'd guessed well. There'd been none of the small-town aloofness he'd been warned of, the you-have-to-be-born-here-to-belong-here mentality. Quite the opposite. He felt so at home with these people he could almost forget he'd been born and raised in an entirely different world.

Turning the corner, there was no missing the extra row of cars in front of the B&B. In the driveway, he looked at the vehicles and recognized several from the trek to the ranch yesterday. "Looks like company," he mumbled to himself. Much like the night before, as he reached the porch, voices and laughter grew louder.

"Oh good, you're home." Meg smiled up at him. "Dinner's almost ready. Want some wine?"

"Maybe later." He was so tired from disposing of more useless stock and unloading the new arrivals, if he had even one glass of wine now he might fall face first in his food. And there was always food. The place was a bed and breakfast, but most nights it was a breakfast and dinner establishment. And if there was cooking involved it could only mean Brooks and his wife were here for dinner. "Hi," he greeted the folks gathered around the huge island, but his eyes zoomed in on one person in particular. Grace. It wasn't good he was so pleased to see her.

Different voices responded and the conversations that had halted at his arrival picked up again.

"Your eyes are going to fall out of your head when you see her." Grace bit into a small stick of celery then waved the remaining stalk in her brother's face. "Your tongue will probably hit the floor too."

DJ cast a glance at his fiancée and grinned knowingly. "She'll be a knock-out."

"She already is," Adam tossed in.

Becky rolled her eyes skyward. "Thanks, Adam, but *she* is right here. I may be a tad distracted, but that doesn't make me invisible. Oh." Becky waved her arm like a kid in a Catholic classroom who wanted the extra credit point. "Which reminds me, Mrs. Peabody came into the clinic today with another stray."

"That woman is going to make 'crazy old cat lady' sound like a compliment one of these days."

"Whatever." Becky rolled her eyes. "But she said that she can't catch the one that was hanging out with the one she brought in to be neutered. She's pretty sure the one who's being so cagey is about to be a mama."

"All right," Adam sighed, "we'll take some of the capture cages out to her house and set them up. Maybe we can entice mama to come and nest."

"And if she's looking for a new home," Chase raised a finger in Adam's direction, "I'll take her."

"Here?" Meg looked startled.

Chase chuckled. "No. For the store."

Now several more faces stared back at him with startled expressions.

"What did I say?"

"Cat and store in the same sentence." Grace shook her head and took a few steps toward where he stood by the island and slid into the empty stool beside him. "Cats and feed stores don't mix."

"Cats eat mice?"

Her eyes opened wide for a second and then a smile bloomed. "They like to play with mice."

"Play?"

"Bat them around like a fussy toy and then come and drop the dead mouse on your doorstep as a prize."

"Sounds like exactly what I need."

"You've got mice," Adam said. Not a question.

"From the looks of it, a whole village."

"You don't want a cat," DJ offered from across the room.

Chase didn't get it. If cats lowered the rodent population, why not a cat in his store? "Don't you guys have barn cats?"

"Yes."

"What am I missing?"

Grace looked at her brothers and with the careful precision of a mother about to explain something very complex and potentially confusing to a small child, placed her hand on his arm and locked gazes with him. "They pee."

Becky giggled, but Meg and Toni looked as confused as he felt. Of course they pee. Every living being did at some point or other.

When he remained silent, she patted his arm again. "On everything."

And then the light bulb went off in his head and flashed on the stacks of hay bundles that customers bought to feed their animals, or pad stalls, or the bags and bags of different feed. Yeah, he got it. Just when he thought the learning curve was becoming manageable, somebody shifted the coordinates.

● ● ● ●

If disappointment had a face, it would belong to Chase Prescott. Grace could almost see his mind mentally kicking himself for not making the connection on his own a lot sooner. "It's an easy thing to overlook if you're used to housecats and litter boxes."

"As much as I hate the idea of using poison, I can't let them continue to infest the warehouse."

"old man Thomas used to put out a treatment. Either he forgot to tell his son about it—"

"Or he didn't really care," Chase finished for her.

"That about sums it up." The whole town knew that the old man's love was with his precious horses. He'd long ago given up on running a decent feed store, but in the middle of God's country, folks tended not to be terribly picky.

The phone in Chase's pocket hummed with vibration and Grace almost missed the wince when he read the caller ID. "Hi, Mom. I thought you and Aunt Cecilia weren't due back for a couple more weeks?" Covering the mouthpiece, he looked to Meg. "This will only be a minute. Can I set the table for you?"

Meg handed him the silverware and he grabbed what he could with his free hand. Once again, Grace felt a little sorry for him.

Juggling the phone with one hand and the silverware with the other left no way to transport the stack of dishes and pile of napkins. Meg mouthed 'I'll get them' and Grace reached out to tap his arm, then pointing at the plates asked with a lift of her brow if he wanted help.

Nodding, Chase set the silverware in front of Grace and picked up the stack of dishes. The guy really was proving to be an outstanding country gentleman. Not that she couldn't have handled the dishes, but his taking on the heavier load was a sweet gesture. The guy was going to make someone a nice husband one day. Snatching up the silverware and napkins, she wondered if New York had any more like him wandering about.

The volume on his cell phone was loud enough that without much effort, Grace could easily follow the conversation.

"That's right, dear," came a voice at the other end of the line. "We're docked in San Juan. Lovely weather. Thought I'd check in on you and see if you've gotten over that silly idea of yours."

Chase set a dish in front of each chair on the one side of the table and glanced up at Grace, before circling around.

Not wanting to eavesdrop, but still being curious, she took her time folding each napkin. Pretty, the way Miss Abernathy had taught them during the county's version of cotillion.

"It's not a silly idea."

"Then you're really going to move to some rural little town and play country boy?"

His gaze darted to Grace and back as he laid down two more plates. "My plans haven't changed."

"You sound just like your father. This is the age of cell phones and internet and self-driving cars. Star Trek is here and the Jetsons are fast approaching. You'll never find Mayberry, Chase."

Again, he looked up at Grace, but this time he reached over for the silverware she had yet to set out. "I think you might be surprised."

"Oh, nonsense. You've been daydreaming with your father since you were five years old. Reality never lives up to the dream.

That's a fact of life. It's why women never really find their Prince Charming."

"Guess it's a good thing I'm not looking for Prince Charming."

Biting back her own amusement, Grace could hear his mother harrumphing on the other end.

"Oh very well. Go ahead and throw away your hard-earned money on some stupid farm with holes in the roof and no hot water. We'll see how long you last with those country bumpkins."

This time, Grace saw unease not at the conversation with his mother, but at the jab directed at the folks in town. Technically, at her too, though she considered herself more a city girl these days.

"I've got a," his gaze shifted to her once again, "dinner date. Have to run."

"Very well, maybe she can talk some sense into you. No woman wants to live in small town USA. Trust your mother."

"Yes, Mom."

"Behave yourself. I love you."

"Love you too." And with those three little words, he tapped the phone and slid it back into his pocket.

"She doesn't know you've already bought the feed store?"

He shook his head.

Grace nodded. "So she has no idea you've been living here for the last few weeks?"

"She and her sister left on back-to-back cruises the day before I came to talk with Mr. Thomas and signed the deal."

For some reason she found that tidbit rather amusing, more specifically how so not amused his mother was going to be when she found out. "So what's the plan? Wait till she docks in homeport to bring her up to date?"

"My mother hasn't been to my apartment in two years. There's a good chance she might not notice I'm gone for at least that long, so long as I answer her calls."

"Ouch." Grace set the last napkin in place. "Sorry."

"Don't be. That's not totally true. My mother has a lot of friends and her social life consists mostly of lunching with said friends and of course dinner as well, but she actually would notice I'd moved away much sooner than two years."

"Two weeks?" Grace ventured.

Chase smiled, a sweet lazy smile that made her want to smile back. "Maybe two months. Give or take a month."

"So if this venture doesn't work out, you can return home and Mom will be none the wiser?" An unexpected pang kicked her center chest at the idea he might not be in Tuckers Bluff the next time she came home. Now she was the dreamer.

"It's not going to wear off. I may not take over the grain and feed market, but it's pretty obvious the customer base isn't going to shop elsewhere, no matter how long my learning curve is."

"So you like it?"

"I do. I think it's time I buy my own place." He chuckled softly. "Don't look so surprised."

Her shock must have been clearly painted on her face. "Sorry. Is your mom right? You want a farm now too?"

Still smiling, Chase shook his head. "No. I never wanted a farm. My dad would talk about horses, or cattle, or even farming, but what he really wanted was to escape the rat race. My mother would tell him with his luck he'd think he was buying the Ponderosa and wind up dragging her to Green Acres."

Grace understood the analogy of the rich ranchers in the TV show *Bonanza* and the city lawyer being shafted in another show of the era, *Green Acres*, but she wondered if his mother was merely practical or like the TV lawyer's wife, spoiled. "And your father hasn't done either?"

His only response was a heavy sigh and a shake of his head. That little lost boy look was reeling her in. She knew she should mind her own business, perform her due diligence as maid of honor for Becky, then get the hell out of Dodge as fast as she could, but how much harm would it really do giving Mr. Suit a little tutoring in country life? "Is Andy going to work tomorrow?"

"Yeah, things are slow for him at the moment."

"Always a good thing for most people."

Smiling again, he nodded. "I suppose it is."

"Why don't you come out to the ranch? The guys saddle up and get moving before sunup to avoid the heat, but if you make it over after breakfast, I can show you a thing or two."

His brows arched high over his eyes.

"About ranching," she added, with a huff. *Men.*

"That would be nice. Is nine good or too early?"

"Nine is fine." And something inside told her if she wasn't careful, teaching this city slicker the ropes could prove to be way more than nice.

CHAPTER NINE

Functioning on less than eight hours sleep was nothing new for Chase, but this morning was different. It wasn't poring over catalogues and internet databases well into the late night hours that had kept him from enough sleep. Thoughts of Grace and what she could teach him, things that had nothing to do with cattle, or horses, or fence mending, had him tossing and turning for hours. Somehow, a woman he'd known for only a few days had completely gotten under his skin. And it made no blinking sense.

Canceling the visit had crossed his mind more than once. Each time he'd reached to call the house, he'd talked himself into going. Truth was, he wanted to go. He wanted to see what he was really made of. Could he stand toe to toe with men who were raised by hard work and made their living off the land? And could he handle a woman who most likely could do the same, if she wanted to? And wasn't that the whole point of his debate? Grace wanted nothing to do with the land, the small town, or any of the things he wanted more than a bigger bank account.

The dashboard clock flashed five minutes to nine as he turned under the scrolling ironwork at the ranch entrance. Damn if this wasn't impressive. He'd been at some of the most exclusive addresses the city and state of New York had to offer and none had made him feel as unworthy as this massive display of man and nature living side by side.

"Good morning." The heavy oak door flew open and Grace stood waving him in. "Did you have time to eat breakfast?"

"More than I wanted. Toni filled me up on pancakes and eggs and bacon and some oatmeal."

"It sticks to the ribs when you're working the fence."

"Is that what we'll be doing?"

"Nope. We're going to saddle the horses, load them into the trailer, then ride out to one of the pastures with the expectant cows and see if there's any signs of trouble."

His first thought was that he wouldn't recognize a cow in distress if it sat on his head, but then he got the distinct feeling there was more to her words than simply a pregnant cow with heartburn. "Something in particular we're looking for?"

Tilting her head slightly to one side, she studied him for a few long seconds. "You really are pretty smart." She turned on her heel and led him to the empty kitchen and out the back door the way he'd gone the other day. "The numbers aren't adding up."

He followed her into the barn and tack room, and waited for more information.

"Not big numbers, and someone could have counted wrong any number of times, but it looks like we're short a few calves."

"Cattle rustling?" He thought that was a thing that went out with gunslingers and saloon girls.

"Maybe."

Carefully he watched Grace explain each piece of gear as she piled his arms high with harnesses, bits, cinches, blankets, and every other little thing needed to saddle a horse. She'd balked when he insisted on carrying the saddles out to the mounting post, but stood her ground when he tried to set it on the horse's back.

"I know you think I can't handle it, but I've been saddling my own horse since I was ten and at this moment if you drop it down too heavily you can do way more harm to the horse than lifting this saddle could possibly do to me."

And as though the thing was as light as a feather, she lifted the saddle up and over the horse's back and set it down, nice and easy. Not slow and careful, just easy. An ease that had clearly come with years of practice. "Nice."

Grace nodded and began moving straps around. "Come here," she said to him. "You don't want it too tight, but you don't want it so loose that it will slide around and the rider finds himself under the horse instead of on it."

He wasn't sure if she was serious or not, but he did as he was told. With the same gentle ease she'd approached the horse with, she took hold of his hand and he had to bite down on his back teeth to keep from reacting to her touch. For a half a second, the way her eyes latched onto his, he thought maybe, maybe this time she'd felt the unusual connection, but without hesitating, she slid his hand under the horse's belly and maneuvered his other hand to tug on the strap.

"See?"

Not trusting himself to avoid saying something stupid, like how soft her hands were, or how nice her perfume smelled, he simply nodded.

At the next horse she stood at his side directing him if he forgot a step, but not once did she touch him again. Had he been right? Had she felt the warming heat? Or was he just indulging his night-time fantasies? Literally shaking his head clear of things he had no business thinking, they finished saddling up the second horse in no time.

Hanging onto the lead, he followed Grace and her horse to where a large trailer was parked. "We're not going to just ride the horses to where the cows are?"

"If we were going to a closer pasture we would. But Finn asked me to check one closer to the south road—"

"South road?"

"The other side of the ranch. We've got somewhere around 100,000 acres. That's lots of land to cross and we don't need to wear out the horses if we don't have to."

"And we don't have to."

"Exactly."

Chase suspected had he needed to load the horses on his own he'd still be standing here tugging and persuading the huge animals to head up the ramp. When Grace did it the whole thing looked so easy.

"Don't feel bad. Ace is smart. He's just testing out the greenhorn."

"Why doesn't that make me feel any better?"

For the first time since they'd entered the barn she grinned at him, doing a pretty good job of not laughing in his face. The tension that had risen up his spine and settled in his shoulders since the first moment her hand had touched his melted away. He could really get used to that smile. Chase was more than sure, when she went back to Dallas to play big business, he was going to miss it.

The first little ways, neither said anything. Grace kept both hands on the wheel as they rode off the property, onto the main road, and down a long ways before reaching a dirt road.

Opening the door, Grace looked at him. "Give me a second to open the gate."

"Need help?"

"Nope. Be right back."

Truth was, he felt odd sitting inside while she moved the heavy gate, but he didn't doubt she made it look easy. Back in the truck, they rode over the cattle rails, the slatted beams in the road to stop the cattle from leaving the pasture if someone should forget to close the gate.

"Okay," she smiled. "You can close it."

At the end of the road, she shifted the truck into park and hopped out. Unloading was seriously easier than loading, or Ace had decided it wasn't worth his time to tease the greenhorn—a greenhorn who was pretty proud of himself for climbing gracefully onto the horse without falling off the other side.

"See those?" She pointed in the distance to his left. Specks of black dashed across a blanket of green and gold. "That's where we're going."

His horse followed Grace's lead. She set the pace. A rather slow pace. Very slow.

"Shouldn't we ride a little faster?"

"Not if you want to walk tomorrow."

"Excuse me?"

"There's no need to gallop. We're not in a hurry."

He nodded.

"And if we trot, unless you've been taught to sit a horse, your tail is going to make you pay."

And he nodded again. The extent of his riding experience had been a few walks around a pen at the dude ranch for his eighth grade class trip. She had a point. "Are there any signs in particular we'll be looking for?"

"Some downed fence line. Damaged fence line. Something that was taken down and then propped up to delay finding it. Tire tracks. Anything suspicious."

The fence and tire tracks he could find. The anything that went with "suspicious" he wasn't so sure of, but he was willing to give it a shot. "It really is beautiful out here."

"It's flat."

"Yes, but beautiful. The way the cows speckle the landscape. The depth of the sky. The silence except for the footsteps of our rides."

"And the incessant mooing of a hundred cows."

"Beats a hundred cabbies and their horns."

"Maybe." She shrugged. "I'd like to see for myself."

"You ever been to New York?"

She shook her head. "Made it to Florida once during spring break. I was supposed to go to New Orleans for a friend from A&M's twenty-first birthday but I came down with bronchitis."

"Haven't had a chance to go back?"

"Nope. Bourbon Street and beignets will have to wait." She glanced his way. "What about you? Been to New Orleans?"

He nodded. "I'm partial to the zeppoles on Arthur Avenue."

"Arthur Avenue?"

"Little Italy, in the Bronx. Same concept as beignets. Fried dough with powdered sugar."

"What about Bourbon Street?"

A smile tugged at his lips before he could hide it. "Not bad."

"Oh yeah." She rolled her eyes at him. "That smile is definitely reflective of a miserable trip to New Orleans."

"I was young. Not very discerning."

Grace looked ahead to the cattle. "I think I'll bump it up on my list."

"Your list?"

"Places I want to go before I'm thirty."

"Ah. I see."

"How are you holding up?"

Wrapping the reins loosely around the horn of his saddle he held his hands out to his side. "See, Mommy, no hands."

"Oh for Pete's sake."

He laughed louder than he should have and retook hold of the reins. He wasn't positive but he thought he saw Ace turn his neck and roll wise brown eyes at him. "What can I say, I should have run away from home and joined a rodeo at a young age."

"That's the circus."

"Yeah, but clowns don't get to play with horses and cows."

"Neither do we."

"I don't know. This feels an awful lot like playing to me." He leaned forward and knew he shouldn't, but he just couldn't resist. Easing his grip on the reins so they hung more loosely, he nudged his heels at the horse's side, clicked his tongue and, taking off, shouted over his shoulder, "Last one to the cows has to has to buy the winner dinner."

CHAPTER TEN

The first thing to cross Grace's mind was that Chase was going to get himself killed. Her second thought was that the city slicker could ride. And fast.

"Oh no, you don't." She had no intention of losing. The crazy man might be able to stay on a galloping horse, but there was no way he could compete with a three-time rodeo champion. Not to mention the youngest child in the family who had always had to keep up with older brothers. Leaning forward and barely pressing her heels into Princess' side, Grace lightly flicked the reins from side to side, gave a familiar yell, and her favorite horse took off like the champion barrel racer she was.

It had been so many years since Grace had flown on Princess. She'd forgotten how great if felt to move as one with such a powerful animal. The wind blowing in her face and the pounding sound of speeding hooves sent an adrenaline burst to every micro cell in her system.

"Whoa," she heard herself yell as she sailed past Chase. Arriving just in front of the herd she eased back to turn around.

Chase came to an out-of-breath stop beside her. "That was amazing." The smile on his face would have been infectious if Grace wasn't already grinning from ear to ear.

"How much riding did you say you'd done?" she asked, slightly out of breath herself.

"Not much." Chase leaned forward and patted his horse's neck.

Grace didn't buy it for a minute, but at the moment she didn't really care. "That wasn't fair. You didn't give us much warning."

"As if you cared. I saw your face light up when you passed me."

She certainly couldn't argue. Chase was right, the second she realized she wasn't just going to have to follow and save his ass, but beat it, was the most exhilarating moment she'd had in a hell of a long time.

Leaning over the saddle horn, still catching his breath and grinning like a fool, Chase cocked his head to one side. "Now what?"

Nearly overcome with the desire to race to the creek and see how Chase handled the swing rope, she tamped down the impulse, took in a long breath to slow her own galloping heart, and scanned the herd. "Now, we go to work."

More than an hour had gone by and they hadn't discovered a single missing cow or calf and no sign of mischief anywhere. A time or two Grace might even have sworn the cows gave her dirty looks for interrupting their afternoon of leisurely grazing or invading the pile of cattle huddled under the solitary patch of shade.

"This time," Grace straightened in the saddle, "we take our time along the fence line back to the truck. Aunt Eileen packed us a nice lunch and I don't know about you, but I'm starved."

"I'm right with you. Worked up a bit of an appetite. I'm so hungry I could eat a…" Chase looked around and swallowed. "Well, I'm just hungry." An apologetic smile crossed his lips and Grace thought for the first time since she'd spotted the too-neat storekeeper staring down at her and his scattered display, that just maybe there really might be a bit of country in this city slicker.

Together they took their time riding the fence line, keeping an eye open for any breaks or other signs of unwanted activity.

Almost back at the truck, Chase came to a halt and slid a little too easily off his mount. "Is this anything?"

Biting down on her back teeth and shaking her head, Grace dropped her reins and climbed off, only a step or two behind Chase. "Damn it." The fence line was intact but a few smoked-to-the-end cigarette butts had been crushed into the ground by the post. "Asshats could have burned the whole damn pasture." She raised her head and looked into the distance where the cows speckled the view. "We'd better tell Finn there might be trouble coming."

"I gather your brothers don't smoke?"

"No one does." Gnawing hunger took a back seat to the possibilities now bouncing around in her mind. And she didn't like any of them.

Chase crouched low and looked at the stomped out butts and the surrounding area. "We should probably call DJ."

"On it." Pulling out her cell she hit speed dial.

"Any chance it's nothing?" Chase asked.

She listened to the ringing phone at her ear. "Always a chance, but damn unlikely."

DJ's voice came on the line. It took all of sixty seconds to explain what they'd found and to be informed to sit tight until he got there. Hungry or not, all they could do now was sit, eat, and wait.

• • • •

An unexpected array of thoughts played in Chase's mind. What if Grace had come out here alone? What if the guy who smoked these cigarettes still stood around watching the herd? What if the guy had tried something with Grace? Suddenly Chase's peaceful Mayberryesque town wasn't as safe and secure as he'd thought.

Walking the short distance to the truck, he and Grace left their horses nearby and settled in for lunch under the shade of the large trailer. Aunt Eileen had packed a cooler with a couple of sandwiches thick enough with cold cuts to be served at a New York delicatessen, along with fruit, chips, and what had to be homemade cookies that could rival the best cookie shops back home.

"You look awfully pensive." Grace took her last bite of sandwich.

"I'm trying to decide if I should propose to your aunt now or wait till she's had time to learn I can be charming and irresistible."

Looking up at him through her lashes, Grace smothered a smile. "Charming and irresistible?"

"So I've been told." He hefted one shoulder.

Grace returned the shrug and ripped open the bag of chips. "I'd wait at least until you're sure you'll be staying."

"I am sure."

"That's right. You said you were thinking of getting a place of your own."

"Yeah." Tossing his napkin into the nearly empty cooler, he sucked in a deep breath and glanced around at the miles of nothing.

Grace scooted her feet close and wrapped her arms around her knees. "I know moving across the country and changing a way of life is a big deal, but that sigh sounded even more ominous."

"Are you always this observant?"

"I'm good at reading people."

"I know you don't want to practice law, but you'd be a great litigator."

She shrugged. "So why the sigh?"

"It's a long story."

"It's a big county. DJ won't be here for a while."

Shifting his weight, he leaned back on his elbows. "My father was a commercial real estate broker. He worked long hard hours. Mom used to say she'd see more of her husband if she'd married a doctor than she did of my father."

Grace lowered her chin onto her knees but gave no indication of what she was thinking.

"I suppose she was right in some ways. He missed a lot of school plays and ball games and charity dinners, but at least he was always home on the holidays. Most of them. He wasn't really an athlete, there wasn't any tossing a ball around, but when he could he'd take me with him to scout out properties or check on construction crews."

"Did you like that?"

"I liked being with my father. One weekend, I must have been around seven, a local station that started playing reruns of the *Andy Griffith Show* had a marathon introduction. Dad made popcorn and we watched for two days. It was the best time my father and I ever spent together." He closed his eyes briefly, considering his own words, then settled his gaze on Grace. "I don't think I've ever admitted that to anyone."

A soft smile appeared on Grace's face. "It's funny what winds up meaning a lot to a child. What about your mom, did she watch with you?"

"Nope. She thought most of the characters too over simplified. Too—"

"Stupid?"

"I didn't say that. Anyhow, watching reruns together became our thing when time allowed. My dad's dream was to retire to Mayberry. Well, someplace like Mayberry. As time flew by and I grew older and the idea of retirement grew more realistic, we'd occasionally talk places to go, what he'd do."

"Let me guess, fishing was top on the list."

Chase laughed. "You'd think, wouldn't you?"

"With the whole father and son whistling while they walked with fishing poles? Yeah, I'd think. He didn't like fishing?"

"He'd never been. I think what he really wanted was the slower pace. Knowing all the neighbors by name."

"Didn't he know your neighbor's names?"

"Most of them, but everyone was always so busy, no one ever really stopped to talk. To visit. That's what Dad wanted."

"Well, he's going to love visiting you here."

Chase swallowed the knot that slithered up his throat. "I think he would have. Working late one night, he had a heart attack. The janitors found him, but it was too late."

Her smile slipped, and sadness filled her eyes. "I'm so sorry. I'd be a basket case if I lost my dad. How long ago has it been?"

Sitting up straight again, he blew out a heavy breath, waiting for the familiar pang of loss to stop hammering at his heart. "It will be two months this coming week."

Grace's eyes rounded with surprise and then softened. "I'm *so* sorry for your loss," she repeated.

"Thanks." He raised one leg and set his arm on his knee. "I was sending out some notifications to the folks on Dad's email account when an email popped up on the screen. Turns out Dad had been keeping tabs on properties for sale all over the country."

"The email was the feed store?"

He nodded. "I almost hit delete without reading it, but something made me open it instead. There wasn't anything about the photos of Main Street that looked even a little like the few shots of Mayberry we saw and yet—"

Grace pulled her knees closer to her chest. "You had to come see for yourself."

"Yeah. I did. My mother and her sister had planned this trip with my aunt months before Dad passed. Aunt Cecilia convinced Mom the trip would do her good. We both figured since Mom and Dad never traveled together, Mom might not feel Dad's absence so much."

"I don't know." Grace paused, tugging at a blade of grass. "My brothers tell me it took Dad a long time to get over my mom's death. I'm not sure I ever have."

"How long ago did she die?" The way Grace's hand froze and her expression dimmed, he wished he hadn't asked.

"She got an infection after I was born. I know it's not the same as with you. I have no memories of my mother at all. Only what others have told me." Her head shot up. "Don't get me wrong. I love my Aunt Eileen, she couldn't have been a better mother to me, but somehow I still miss my mom."

Grace didn't need to say anything more, he got it. He'd had his father all of his life and yet in many ways, he too missed the dad he hadn't had. "I'm sorry." *Really sorry.*

In the quiet of pasture the sound of an engine carried to them before he could see where it came from.

Grace looked up in the direction of the soft roar. "That's probably DJ."

Pushing to his feet, Chase glanced up and hoped it wasn't trouble. Turning back to Grace, he took a step in her direction.

Grace sprang up at the same moment he leaned forward to offer a hand and her feet scrambled beneath her, nearly toppling her over.

"Whoa." Moving a half step closer, he wrapped his hands around her arms to steady her. The only problem was she now stood stock still only inches away from him. Close enough for him to feel the warmth of her breath and count the beats of her heart.

A sane man would have let go. Taken a step back. Ignored the fire in her deep blue eyes. Remembered the engine fast approaching. What was left of his mind knew that. Understood that. Too bad his mouth had a mind of its own.

CHAPTER ELEVEN

One side of Grace's mind screamed *danger danger* while the other side thought *oh hell yeah*. Before she could make any conscious decision to back up or fall forward, soft firm lips danced over hers, pressing, easing, fanning heat and teasing yearning with a skill that had her arms around his neck and her body snug against his, eager to learn more.

A soft moan floated between them—hers, his, who knew. Air rumbled around her and the sane side of her mind reminded her that the rumble wasn't the air but an approaching car. Her brother's approaching car. And fool that she was, she still didn't want to stop.

"Grace," Chase murmured against her lips. Releasing his hold on her hips, he took a step back and sucked in a long deep breath. "I probably shouldn't have done that, but…" A slow lazy grin tilted the corners of his mouth upward in a crooked smile. A very sexy crooked smile. "I'm not going to apologize."

If she'd been a peacock she would have spread her feathers and strutted across the field.

A police department SUV pulled up behind the trailer and DJ hopped out. "What's going on?"

For a split second panic at being caught by her older brother in the arms—really nice arms—of a man she barely knew, slammed her in the rib cage. The casual way her brother waltzed over told Grace he hadn't seen, or noticed, the kiss. And a good thing, too. She hadn't a clue what the hell was going on between her and Chase; explaining it to someone else would be more than difficult. Right about now redirecting her thoughts to potential cattle rustling struck her as just fine.

Chase was the first to turn and face DJ. "Over by the fence."

It took a couple of beats for Grace to get with the program and follow the other two back to where they'd found evidence of a potential intruder. It wasn't like her to be left a bit stunned by a mere kiss, but stunned she was. And even more surprising to her was that she wanted to do it again.

Over by the fence, more quickly than she would have thought, her brother scooped up the cigarette butts into an evidence bag and the three took another look around the area for more signs of two-footed life. With no other indication of trespassers around, DJ was as hesitant as they were to presume this was somehow related to the few missing cows. "I haven't any idea how long these butts have been here," DJ said, "and I'm not willing to take a wild guess either."

To Grace it was obvious they couldn't have been out in the open air for all that long or they'd have been more deteriorated, but even with the lack of rain in recent years, she wasn't willing to take any guesses. Minding her own business and keeping her thoughts to herself, she loaded the horses while DJ gave the place one last look over.

"Nothing else," DJ practically sighed.

Grace set a hand on her brother's arm. "Maybe it's nothing more than some kids finding a quiet place to sneak a few drags."

"Maybe." He didn't look all that convinced.

"What about Dale? Any more news on him?"

"Still stable but it's been long enough that the doctors are more hopeful."

"Good." Grace stepped back with a smile. "Good."

Whether it was the cigarettes or Dale that kept concern etched on his face, Grace didn't know.

DJ started for his SUV. "I'll follow y'all back to the ranch. I want to talk to Finn. Connor too." Turning, he paused by Chase. "Want to ride back with me?"

Chase cut her a sideways glance. She could almost read his mind weighing the pros and cons to not riding back to the ranch in the same confined space with her. She, on the other hand, had nothing to consider. She was delighted to have a little time to clear her head of the kiss and the tingly sensations still humming inside her. "Go on, you two can have a male bonding moment."

DJ merely rolled his eyes seconds before slipping on his shades and looking all police chief on her.

Driving back to the ranch alone, all the different things she and Chase had said and mentioned over the last few days sprinted through her mind, tumbling together and one by one taking a backseat to the memory of a few minutes ago. If she couldn't shake the feel of Chase's mouth on hers when he was nowhere near her, she didn't have the foggiest idea how the heck she was supposed to ignore the vivid memory when they once again stood side by side. And in front of her aunt no less. A woman with instincts sharper than a mama bear and a dangerous penchant for matchmaking. By the time she pulled up to the ranch Grace had decided that decisions were highly overrated. There was something to be said for go-with-the-flow and since it looked like this city boy was good and countrified, she was going to do just that. Go with the flow.

Keys in hand, she'd set one foot outside the truck when DJ appeared at her side. "Looks like Finn's in the barn. If you want to head inside with Hannah, I can take care of your mount."

"Is Dad inside too?"

DJ nodded.

"Y'all are impossible." She hopped out of the truck and slammed the door behind her. "You don't want Aunt Eileen to know there's a potential problem with rustlers?"

"All we know is the cattle count is slightly off. No sense in worrying her."

She stopped toe to toe with her brother. "Aunt Eileen is not a frail flower. All of you did the same thing when Brittany landed on your doorstep. She handled the news just fine and she can handle this." Grace stabbed at her finger into her brother's chest. "I'll let you take care of the horses and teach Mr. Feed Store how we do it, but when you're done, everyone back in the house to discuss this *with* Aunt Eileen."

The way DJ's jaw tightened, she was fully aware he didn't want to, but the resignation in his eyes told her he knew damn well she was right. This wasn't turn of the last century. Women did not need protection from reality.

"Agreed," she blurted out, tired of waiting for a response.

DJ didn't utter a sound, he merely nodded and walked away with Chase.

"Macho hot shots," she mumbled under her breath, stomping onto the porch. Sucking in a deep calming breath, she turned the knob and softening her steps, searched out the folks in the kitchen.

"Oh, lord I didn't think about that." Elbow on the table, two fingers rubbing her temple, Connor's wife Catherine sat staring at a pile of papers.

Hannah pulled a nearby chair out and slid into the seat, large mug in hand. "The logistics can be a nightmare."

"So I see," Catherine muttered.

Hannah blew over the rim of the mug. "Then you have the issue of temperament."

"Whose temperament?" Aunt Eileen came out of the pantry carrying several cans. "Not Connor. There's no better man to work with, human or beast."

"The horses." Hannah looked up. "Just because a horse is a docile ride doesn't mean it will be a good therapy horse. Especially for the physically handicapped. Some horses are too sensitive. They slow up or change their gait so the rider never has to fully use all their muscles for balance—"

"Which defeats the purpose." Catherine let out another sigh. "Connor and I have been working on state-of-the-art facilities for children with physical disabilities, but we failed to consider parents."

"Or caretakers," Hannah added.

Aunt Eileen stood with a can opener in one hand and a can in the other. "How did none of us consider that?"

"Don't be too hard on yourself. Most folks who haven't dealt with a disability underestimate what's involved."

"Like running a non-profit. I anticipated it would be a damn nuisance to set up but considered the objective well worth the effort. Turns out running it is a legal morass that will suck away time I don't have. And now we can't even do what we set out to do."

"Why not?" Grace knew Catherine was a damn good litigator and smart enough to work out the challenges of running a non-profit, but wasn't quite following the current problem.

"Equine therapy camps for low income children and teens with issues is a great idea for a day camp," Hannah explained, "but not so easy for a sleepover camp."

"I think we're going to have to rethink this." Catherine pressed her lips tightly together and, still staring at the plans, shook her head ever so slightly. "I just wanted to help more kids like Stacey. Kids whose parents are losing hope with traditional therapy. Or who haven't any hope at all."

"Stacey didn't have a physical disability," Grace stated the obvious.

Hannah nodded her head. "My point exactly."

Silence hung loudly in the air. Staring at the three women by the table, Aunt Eileen had stopped opening cans. Hannah held onto her mug, but made no effort to continue drinking. Focused on the plans in front of her, Catherine looked absolutely miserable. And Grace had nothing productive to add. It was as if she and the others were watching Catherine's dream crumbling. Suddenly, what to do about a little—okay, a knock your socks off—kiss in the middle of a field from a hot guy who wanted all the things she'd spent seven years avoiding, didn't seem like such a big deal anymore.

• • • •

"Well at least the expression 'ridden hard and put away wet' makes a hell of a lot more sense to me now." Chase hadn't had even the slightest clue about all that was involved in caring for a horse after going for a ride. A typical city guy, he'd expected the reverse of taking the animal out. Saddle it up to go for a ride and take the saddle off after bringing him home. Nowhere in his expectations had walking, brushing, feeding, watering, or cleaning out hooves come into play. Though he had learned that Grace's and his horse didn't need walk-off time in the paddock since the riding along the fence line had been slow and easy, apparently that was not the case with Finn and his father's horse. Their rides had worked up a sweat and were still damp when they returned to the barns. Not wanting the animals to develop any of the things explained to him, from joint inflammation to colic and bacterial infections, the horses were walking it off much like a runner after a race.

"Now what?" Lips pressed tightly, eyes pensive, Sean Farraday shifted his gaze from the evidence bag to his police chief son.

"I send the butts to the lab for analysis and we see what comes back." DJ cast his glance from brother to father and back. "While I'm waiting I'll have a little chat with some other ranchers, maybe ride a line or two myself nearest the main roads. See if I spot anything else suspicious."

Bobbing his head, the senior Farraday slapped his son on the shoulder. "Sounds good. You let us know if you want some help with that fence riding."

"Thanks, but not yet. I don't want to alarm anyone."

"You know, Ken Brady mentioned something to me a couple of weeks ago at the café. It's what got us looking closer."

"I remember. I'm going to start with him."

"So who's going to break the news to Aunt Eileen?" Finn asked.

"Not yet," Sean said softly, shaking his head. "I want to know more before we get her riled up."

Chase almost felt like pulling up a chair to sit and watch the rest of the conversation. If Grace had been his sister, he'd be arguing her case about now. The fact that he agreed with her being irrelevant, what he wasn't so sure of was if DJ agreed or not. Or what Finn thought. But he did know so far the score was one to Grace and one to her father.

"About that," DJ cleared his throat. "Grace doesn't want to hide this from her. I think if we don't mention it, Grace will."

"She's right," Finn shrugged. "Aunt Eileen is not a daft old woman nor a naïve youngster. I don't want to be on the receiving end of another tongue lashing when she finds out we kept something this important from her."

"Besides," DJ addressed his dad, already hinting at whose side he'd be on. "So far we aren't sure of anything. There's no imminent danger. No threat to Aunt Eileen or anyone up here at the house, but there is enough suspicion for her to keep her eyes and ears open."

Sean Farraday shook his head. "Knowing her, she'd mount a horse and go hunting down all the fence lines on her own."

"And that's a bad thing why?" Finn crossed his arms.

Chase was loving this familial dialogue. Growing up an only child, he'd had no experience with this, and frankly none of his friends had families this down to earth. He wondered if Grace appreciated having a family this close knit. Or had any idea how much her brothers respected her to fight on her side. A telling gesture considering she was the youngest, and a girl to boot. Not that it seemed to matter out here. So far he'd been given the distinct impression that equality was far less of an issue in the rural west, where everyone shared and shared alike, than in the city where folks were battling about the glass ceiling.

"Finn's right," DJ put in. "You let Grace ride the line alone today."

"Excuse me," Chase raised a finger at DJ, fishing for a little levity, "she wasn't exactly alone."

"You know how to use a gun?" DJ deadpanned.

Chase shook his head.

"Then she might as well have been alone." DJ turned back to his father. "What's it going to be?"

Thin muscles at the edge of the older man's jawline twitched with discontent. The decision wasn't coming easy.

"You know we'll stand by your decision, Dad," Finn spoke up, "but I do think Grace is right. Aunt Eileen doesn't need protecting from life."

Their father blew out a long sigh. Chase was pretty sure he saw the man's muscles tense with effort. "Very well. Y'all are old enough to have your say. Three to one seems pretty clear."

"You sure?" DJ asked and his brother nodded.

"Yep," their dad sighed. "I may not like it, but that doesn't mean y'all aren't right."

And with something that simple, the men walked out of the barn toward the house. Chase's mother wouldn't believe him, but he just might have found his Ponderosa family in Mayberry after all.

CHAPTER TWELVE

From where she stood in the kitchen Grace could see the men coming back from the barn. Her heart had no business kicking into fast gear. It was only one kiss. And the fact that she so wanted to do it again was the biggest reason why she shouldn't. She had a plan. A good plan. Though it might need some tweaking. Chase Prescott was too damn tempting for her own good. Sticking around the ranch for a few months to study for the bar was looking less and less like a good idea. She'd better let her roommate know she'd be coming home after the wedding to study.

"Oh, dear. I think he's going to leave." Aunt Eileen turned off the water, grabbed a dish rag to wipe her hands, shuffled across the kitchen and threw open the back door. "You're not letting our guest leave without supper, are you?"

An expression akin to the day after a stock market crash slipped from her dad's face and a soft chuckle and sweet smile took its place. "Of course not Eileen."

Chase looked to her father as though that was the first he'd heard of staying for supper, but when he turned back toward the house, he was smiling as broadly as her dad. The back door creaked open wider and one by one the men filed in, each hanging their hats on a hook except for Chase. He glanced at the hook and she could almost see the wheels of his mind turning. *How stupid would he look in a Stetson?* Unfortunately, the answer rolling around her head wasn't the expected, but instead, *damn hot.*

"What are all the glum faces about?" Sean headed straight to the fridge and poured his customary after work glass of milk. For years he'd drunk the stuff due to ulcers. By now Grace figured he drank it out of sheer habit than for medicinal purposes.

"Just a few setbacks," Catherine answered. "We're going to have to rework the foundational idea for the therapy camp."

"Rework how?" Finn pulled a beer from the mudroom refrigerator.

"Accommodating handicapped children and their parents or caregivers is going to be an expensive challenge."

DJ accepted the beer his brother handed him, his eyes slightly narrowed. "So you're thinking what? Emotional disabilities? Autism?"

"Sort of." Hannah waved her hand back and forth. "Autistic children rarely deal well with changes. Just sending them to a strange city with people they don't know could be severely traumatic."

DJ nodded. "Of course. I hadn't even thought about that. Definitely not a good thing."

"See what I mean?" Catherine gathered all the papers and slid them into a folder.

DJ took a long swallow and the set the bottle on the counter behind him. "What about adults with PTSD?"

Catherine's head shot up.

"Marines," Hannah volunteered. "We work with quite a few veterans. Not just PTSD. Lots come home with a variety of injuries that can be helped by equine therapy."

For the first time since Grace had come through the door, Catherine's expression regained a flicker of hope.

But by the steely-eyed gaze with which DJ stared at the two women seated at the kitchen table, Grace knew exactly what he was thinking. "Dale? You're thinking of helping cops with PTSD."

DJ nodded, twisted behind him to retrieve the bottle, and without taking a sip picked at the damp label. "Something like that."

Her cousin Jamie stood at the back door kicking his boots clean. "I think it's a great idea."

"Me too." Connor scooted around his cousin to hang his hat. "What little I heard."

"That dirt looks good on you, boy." Sean smiled at his nephew. "When are you going to give up that city job and go home to help your Da?"

Jamie smiled the same lazy smile all the Farraday men had. "Nope. It's okay for a day in the stables with my favorite cuz—"

"I thought I was your favorite cousin." DJ bit back a smile.

Jamie pulled a beer from the fridge and, waving one in the air at Connor, waited until his cousin shook his head at the offer to put the second beer back and twist the top off his own. "I've got a lot of favorite cousins."

"Charmer, is what he is." Aunt Eileen slid over and on tippy-toe gave her nephew a peck on the cheek. Didn't matter that they weren't related by blood, not even by marriage. To Aunt Eileen, all Farradays were family. "Do you really have to head back tomorrow?"

Jamie slung an arm around their aunt. "'Fraid so. I'm on the schedule for Thursday night."

"And if I want to keep my job I need to be back by tomorrow afternoon," Hannah added, "so we'll be up and out of here at first light with the rest of the family."

"Maybe what we need is a bar here in town," Chase suggested. Several startled heads swiveled around to face him. "Or... maybe not."

"Actually," Finn moved to sit at the table, "you wouldn't be the first to suggest we need a place to buy a beer or take a turn on the dance floor without driving to Butler Springs."

"I was actually thinking of a nice restaurant, but I can see where a bar with a dance floor would work."

Jamie laughed and shook his head. "That'll be the day."

DJ shrugged. "Never know. Prohibition was repealed a long time ago."

Just about everyone at the table laughed at that. Not that it would make any difference. The town council was pretty set in their ways.

"And as long as we're moving people into town," her dad took a seat by Finn, "Chase here is ready to set down roots."

"Buying a feed store wasn't setting down roots?" Aunt Eileen teased.

"Well yeah," Finn smiled, "but he can't stay at the B&B forever. We were talking in the barn and it got me thinking." He looked at DJ. "What shape is the old foreman's house in on Adam's property?"

"The hospital?" Catherine asked. "Or are you thinking the apartment over the clinic?"

"Wait a minute," DJ leaned forward, with an exaggerated expression of surprise. "Is my fiancée moving out of the apartment and I don't know it?" He was of course teasing. He and everyone else at the table knew damn well that he would be moving in with Becky after the wedding.

"Hold on." Chase had shifted his attention from person to person as each suggestion was offered, and now held up his hand. "Hospital? Clinic? Do you guys know something I don't?"

"Relax," Grace said with a grin, "Adam and Ethan's fiancée, Allison, are remodeling an antebellum ranch estate into a hospital for locals. They're leasing the land to ranchers but hadn't decided what to do with the foreman's house."

Chase's face lit with interest. "Where is it?"

"Not far from town," DJ said. "But I haven't seen it up close in ages."

"I'm sure Adam would be happy to let you walk through it," Aunt Eileen chimed in, then turned to Grace. "As a matter of fact, we'll be playing cards tomorrow at the café—"

"When was that decided?" Grace cut her aunt off. She didn't know what or why, but she smelled an awfully convenient rat.

"Just recently, dear. But you can pick up the key from Adam then take Chase to look." Smiling like the proverbial cat with a bowl of cream, her aunt turned to Chase. "Don't you think that's an excellent idea?"

Slightly wide eyed, Chase looked momentarily at Grace and then back at her aunt. "Yes, I'll have to check with Andy—"

"Oh, Andy is thrilled to have extra work. He'll be fine with it, I can assure you." Aunt Eileen returned her attention to the simmering pot on the stove. "Great idea, Finn."

Finn shrugged at Grace. DJ smothered a smile. Connor nodded his head and at the center of it all, Chase seemed all too pleased. Grace couldn't help but think that getting this wedding over with and getting herself back to Dallas couldn't happen fast enough.

• • • •

For Chase, the amazing burst of stars was a literal bright spot of driving from the ranch back to town at night. Every evening the clear skies of West Texas turned from deep blue to dark black and the stars sparkled like diamonds on velvet. So many bright lights that the sky almost gleamed white. An incredible sight.

"You would love it here, Dad." Everything in him wished his father was still around to share this moment. The day his father died, Chase stopped chasing the brass ring. He'd learned everything about business and hard work and dreams from his father. And how one wasn't worth much without the other. "You'd like Grace too."

The look on her face when that dog knocked her into the cardboard point of sale display was priceless. The reaction when her brothers explained the dog was the stray the whole town had credited with matching her brothers and their mates was twice as memorable. But his favorite of her many faces by far was the dazed expression this afternoon when he'd kissed her. He wouldn't mind seeing what face she'd make if he kissed her again. This time with little chance of interruption.

The lights of Tuckers Bluff drew closer in the distance, shifting his thoughts to where this place was that Brooks was redoing. Except for the few times he'd driven to the Farraday ranch, he'd not explored out of town. Curiosity almost had him ignoring the turn on the street to the B&B and continuing across the small town and out to find the hospital land, but another part of him was seriously looking forward to seeing it for the first time with Grace. And wasn't that an interesting turn of events? After all these years he'd finally found someone who intrigued him in a million different ways and she was just as eager to get out of town as he was to settle in.

Pulling into the driveway of the B&B, he took one last look at the stars. The plan had been to call Brooks to talk about the property, but if he recognized the car in front, it looked like the conversation had come to him. Locking the car door out of habit more than necessity, he made his way up the porch steps and into the house. Adam and Meg were nestled on the oversized sofa in the casual living area. Brooks and Toni sat across on the loveseat.

Meg was the first to spot him and pushed herself upright. "How was the work day at the ranch?"

"Very informative." He hesitated to interrupt, but really wanted to talk about the house.

Brooks leaned forward and gestured for Chase to take a seat. "Finn called."

Chase should have known the brothers would have cleared the way for him.

"Says you're ready to settle down more permanent like."

He glanced at Adam and Meg. "Nothing against the B&B—"

"Of course not. You can't live here forever." Meg pushed to her feet. "Did you leave any room for dessert?"

Adam turned to his wife. "You're joking?"

Lifting her hand, palm-out, at Chase, she said, "Never mind, Adam's right. What was I thinking? How about an herbal tea?"

"That would be great." Chase nodded as Meg gestured to Brooks and Toni.

"None for me," Brooks said.

Toni shook her head. "Me neither."

"Only three cups coming up then."

Chase watched Meg leaving the room and wondered if he had ever seen his parents as happy together as the couples in the Farraday family.

"If you're thinking of staking a claim, she's taken." Only the twinkle in Adam's eyes reassured Chase the comment was made in jest.

"Sorry."

Smiling, Adam waved him off, confirming the comment was only teasing.

Brooks rested his forearms on his thighs. "The foreman's house is in pretty rough shape. It's been abandoned for decades now."

"What are your plans for it?"

"We don't really have any. Toni and I have discussed maybe keeping it for ourselves, but we decided we'd rather build something a little bigger. The other option was using it for doctor's offices or something of the sort if the hospital gets too big or busy, though that seems highly unlikely."

"So you'd consider selling it?" Now, excitement truly began to rise.

Nodding, Brooks leaned back again. "Maybe. It's far enough away that everyone would have their privacy, but it's close enough to the main road that we could easily allocate its own boundaries. What are you looking for, five, ten acres?"

Five. Ten. "Uh, actually I was thinking one would be huge."

Adam laughed. "I suppose if it were in the city it would be. You sure you wouldn't rather buy something here in town?"

"Is there anything in town?" Meg came in carrying the customary wooden tray with tea pot and cups.

"Actually," Chase scooted forward to reach the cups, "I wouldn't mind a nice Victorian like this."

Adam and Brook's brows arched like mirrored images.

"Well, not necessarily this big, but something with architectural interest. What's the Foreman's house like? Brick ranch?"

"Nope," this time Brooks replied. "That sucker was built a hell of a lot longer ago than that. More craftsman in style."'

"Really?"

Brooks smiled. "Really."

"Would you mind letting me borrow the keys? Go tomorrow sometime and take a look?"

"That would be hard," Meg said with a smile, shaking her head when Chase's smile slipped. "House doesn't have any locks."

Settling back next to his wife again, Brooks shook his head at his sister-in-law. "Go take a look, see if you like it and then we'll talk some more."

"Thanks." Chase resisted the urge to do a fist pump like a stoked teen. For reasons he couldn't explain, buying his own home in this Mayberry look-alike felt more real than anything else he'd done so far. "I think that's already the plan. For Grace to show me where it is."

"Makes sense," Meg nodded. "If you can see past the problems, I'm sure you'll love it."

Something in the way his hostess' eyes twinkled told him what she'd just said had nothing to do with housing.

CHAPTER THIRTEEN

"**F**our ladies. Read 'em and weep." Eileen spread her cards on the table and scooped in her chips.

"So explain to me again," Sally May tossed her cards onto the table. "Why did we get a last minute call to meet here this morning?"

Despite being the only occupied table on this side of the café midway between breakfast and lunch, Eileen leaned forward and lowered her voice. "I wanted an excuse to come into town with Grace."

"Why? So she could play real estate agent?" Ruth Ann gathered the remaining cards from the table. "I suppose as an attorney she's allowed to do that."

"We could use a real estate agent in town." Sally May grabbed half the deck to help Ruth Ann shuffle.

"Oh, for land's sake." Dorothy shook her head. "Y'all have to know this is about the new guy and Grace."

Ruth Ann stopped shuffling and stared at Eileen. "Did you bet?"

"Who cares if she's in on the pool?" Dorothy blurted. "What she wants is to keep them close. Or closer."

"And that abandoned old house seems as good a place as any." Eileen couldn't help but grin. She loved watching her babies fall in love and so far the dog hadn't gotten it wrong.

"Oh sure," Dorothy cut the deck. "Nothing like dirt, dust, cobwebs and field mice for a romantic setting."

"Mice?" Ruth Ann stopped mid-deal. "Ugh."

"Hmm. I hadn't thought about that." Eileen might have been romanticizing the scenario a tad. But Grace and the new hunk in town had spent most of yesterday afternoon alone together and while Eileen got the feeling things were shifting between the pair, she needed more—and fast. There was no telling how long Grace would stay in town and once she was back in Dallas who knew when she'd be back.

"If you aren't in the betting pool," Ruth Ann dealt the first card, "I don't see why it matters. All the others got together just fine without your help."

"Not true," Dorothy picked up a card. "Eileen concocted that little-too-sick-to-get-out-of-bed scenario for Ethan."

Eileen smiled and reached for her cards. "And it worked too."

"I don't know," Sally May rearranged her cards. "I bet they would have gotten together anyhow. I mean, you can manipulate a lot of things, but you can't control people falling in love."

Polly of the Cut and Curl came hurrying in the front door. "Mabel Berkner canceled at the last minute."

"Well what has you in such a rush?" Abbie came to a stop beside the table.

"Heard Grace is showing the greenhorn the foreman's house out by the new clinic." Polly grinned. "I want to change my bet."

Abbie put her two fingers together and whistled lightly.

A carafe of coffee in one hand and a pie plate in the other, Shannon spun around.

"Bring the notebook," Abbie called out.

Shannon nodded, turned back around to fill her customer's cup, then set the plate down and ran into the kitchen. Before anyone could blink she was hurrying up to the table. "Who wants in?"

"You're taking the bets?" Dorothy's eyes widened. "I thought this was Burt's idea?"

Shannon giggled. "Well, he wanted to get in on the pool and I was the only neutral party available."

All eyes at the table turned to Abbie. "Hey, if the dog had knocked me into Chase Prescott, I'd bet on him too." Lifting her fists onto her hips, she cast her glance from one card-playing club member to the other. "Well?"

The four women looked to each other.

Dorothy shrugged. "Grace. She's too hardheaded."

"Yep," Sally May nodded. "Grace."

Ruth Ann shook her head. "Hot Stuff all the way."

"I'm shifting from Grace to Hot Stuff too," Polly beamed. "I hadn't counted on so many encounters of the close kind."

"Looks like me, my niece and her future husband are the only three people in town besides Shannon here who haven't placed a bet."

Shannon smothered a grin.

"You're kidding?" different voices muttered.

Shannon shook her head slowly and her grin widened. "Both of them."

"Well I'll be damned," Eileen leaned back in the chair. "Wonder if either of them is on the dog's side."

All heads turned to Shannon. Her expression didn't falter. "Don't look at me. Last thing I need is to be tossed in jail for insider trading."

"I don't think the Securities and Exchange Commission cares about our town's little pool."

Shannon shrugged, stepped away, and over her shoulder called. "Maybe. Maybe not."

And maybe, Eileen considered, that sweet matchmaking mutt could pull this one off without any help from her. Then again...

• • • •

"These are fantastic." Andy handed Chase another of the new halters. "Where'd you get the hand roped ones?"

"Last week a gal came in with them. She looked like she could use the money so I bought them. Hadn't planned on putting them for sale but after talking to Grace—"

"You two are hitting it off pretty well it seems."

How did he answer that? Did having enough chemistry between them to self-combust even when the party of the first part had no intention of sticking around with the party of the second part, count as hitting it off pretty well? "All the Farradays have been very helpful."

"But you do like her?" Andy coaxed.

Chase hung the last harness and studied Andy a second. Where had all this curiosity about him and Grace come from? "The pool."

At least Andy had the decency to look embarrassed as recognition dawned. "I know you've been at the ranch a bit the last few days, but now that you two are going house hunting—"

"I'm going house hunting. We're not moving in together."

"Yeah," Andy shifted his feet awkwardly, "but still, if y'all are hitting it off. I mean, it's not like you asked Meg to show you around."

"I didn't ask Grace either."

"Oh." Frowning, Andy took a step back. "Then if you don't like her, I don't have to change my bet."

Another damned if he did and damned if he didn't question. The warning about the expiration date on the milk carton scrolled across his mind. If he gave any hint he liked Grace, he was pretty sure the entire town would not only know it, they'd probably chip in for the reception. On the other hand, if he said he wasn't interested, that too would probably reach Grace's ears within the hour and could annihilate any chance he had of seeing where this thing might go.

The jingle of the door chime saved him from having to give any response. In the standard West Texas attire of jeans, boots, and button down shirt, Grace entered the store. What he wouldn't give to trade places with those curve-hugging jeans for just an hour... or more.

"Hey, Miss Grace." Andy bobbed his chin.

"Hi, Andy. How's your mom's arthritis doing?"

"Not bad. She cut back on potatoes and her ankles aren't swelling so much."

"Good. I'm glad it worked. Make sure to tell her I asked about her."

"Will do." Andy turned to his boss. "I'll take these empty boxes out back."

"Thanks." Chase redirected his thoughts to the business at hand. "We shouldn't be long."

"Ready then?" Grace asked.

"All set." He skirted around her and held the door open. From time to time he'd do that in New York, but more often than not women would reach for the handle before he could. He liked that Grace didn't mind the simple courtesy.

Walking to the car, Grace waved a hand at his new boots. "Comfortable, aren't they?"

"Not yet, but I'm told once I break them in, I'll never want to wear anything else."

Grace chuckled. "That would have to be Sister."

"It was." He nodded. "Sissy is responsible for the jeans. Told me if I wanted to fit in I'd have to stop looking like I just stepped off a yacht."

"I guess she thinks khakis are boating attire."

Chase opened the driver's side door. "She was right about one thing, business casual doesn't really fit in with working a feed store."

"No," she chuckled, "it doesn't." Buckled in and the engine started, Grace backed out and turned south out of town. "I spoke with Brooks this morning. Seems the idea of selling the foreman's house is growing on him."

"Good." It was growing on Chase too.

"It's not far outside of town. You'd be able to get back and forth to work without losing much time."

"Getting around here doesn't take much time no matter what. Even out to the ranch. It's over sixty miles but in a big city that's going to take a hell of a lot longer than just under the hour it takes on these empty roads."

Smiling, Grace stepped on the gas. "Or even less than that for some."

With Miss Leadfoot driving, they reached the hospital project in no time. "Wow. It's like looking at Tara."

"It does have that *Gone with the Wind* air, doesn't it? It always reminded me of the big house on that old TV show with Barbara Stanwyck. What was it called?"

"*Big Valley*."

"That's right."

The place looked a bit rough around the edges. There were signs of construction—piles of materials inside a temporary chain link fence. Now that he took a second look, he realized the exterior had been scraped in preparation for painting. "When will it be ready?"

"Good question. Getting contractors to come all the way out here isn't easy. Folks get tired of commuting from Butler Springs pretty fast and there's no real motel anywhere closer either."

Which meant there wouldn't be too many folks around to help him either.

"That's one of the reasons most of the work renovating the B&B was done by the family over a few months."

"Even you?" For some crazy reason the idea of Grace wielding a hammer made his blood stir. Maybe it was some warped *Green Acres* fantasy. He'd have to figure that one out another time.

"Even me. Raised on a ranch there's no gender bias. We all did our share, but with Meg and Adam's place, I wasn't around often enough to do much more than help paint the kitchen."

"That's more than most people would do." Certainly more than his mother would ever have attempted. "There really is so much of nothing all around us."

"Ain't that the truth."

Now he wished he hadn't commented on the vast landscape. The last thing he wanted to do at the moment was point out the things that pushed Grace away.

"Here you are."

In the distance, he could see the small wooden structure taking form. Closing the gap, the wooden framed home was indeed a typical craftsman. Could his world possibly get any better?

CHAPTER FOURTEEN

No matter how many times Grace may have driven by the rickety old house and other abandoned structures scattered about the county, she never got over how easily anything left unattended could rot and fall apart in the baking Texas sun. "Definitely counts as rough around the edges."

"Just needs some love."

The way Chase grinned up at the massive front porch under the typical gabled roofs and broad eaves, with the same reverence and awe he might display in front of the Taj Mahal, made her do a double take. What the hell did he see in this tattered old house?

"Are you coming?" Chase stood on the front porch.

So absorbed in how unkempt the house was, she hadn't noticed him sprint up the steps. "Yes. Of course." She hurried up after him. The porch was at least ten or more feet deep and twice as wide. Funny, but as dilapidated as it had appeared from the front yard, standing here beside him, for a split second she could see dark green rockers to one side and a wooden porch swing at the other. She could almost picture someone on the swing sipping on a fresh lemonade.

"Grace?"

"Oh." She shook the odd thoughts free and sidled up beside Chase. "It's unlocked."

His hand already on the knob, shaking his head, Chase turned his wrist and pushed in the door. Inside, he scanned the room from left to right and his head shifted from side to side again. "Amazing. If this were any place else there would be holes in the walls, pipes missing," he shrugged, "maybe even light fixtures gone, a little graffiti here or there, and I bet..." He crossed the room and disappeared down the hall before reappearing. "Yep. Kitchen is intact. Old and leaning, but intact."

It was the floors that had caught Grace's eye. The original narrow oak planks were dusty and tired but she had a feeling a good cleaning and buffing might be enough to bring them back to life. She could easily see the gleaming floors under a couple of love seats, an easy chair, a few dark wood pieces for contrast and lacy sheers at the windows. Instead of dingy gray that might have once been white, the walls boasted a buttery yellow with bright white trim. She could see it all so vividly that, for a few seconds, she forgot she was standing in an empty room.

"I love it." Chase beamed.

"All you've seen is two rooms. How can you know you love it?"

Casually hefting one shoulder, he shrugged and turned. "Feels right."

"Thought women are supposed to be the ones with intuition," she muttered and followed him down the hall past the kitchen and into the first bedroom on the left. Nothing very big, but not really small either.

"Could make a good office or guest room," he said before moving on.

Across the hall, the room at the end had to be the master. Clearly several feet larger, the room had windows on two sides, lots of fresh sunshine, and when Grace blinked she saw an antique four-post bed with a wedding ring quilt and a big gray dog asleep at the foot. Squeezing her eyes tight, she focused on the space between the windows and blew out a relieved breath at the empty space.

"Something wrong?" Chase moved in close. "You look a little pale."

"Nope. All is well." She stepped back. The last thing she wanted with her mind playing tricks on her was for him to reach out and touch her in any way. "Lots of doors." Taking a broad step forward, she opened one door. "Wow, this is pretty nice for a house that's at least a hundred years old." The closet wasn't grand by today's walk-in standards, but considering a lot of these old houses didn't have closets at all, this one was positively royal.

"And here's another." Holding the door open, Chase leaned in to look. "Not as big, but still technically a walk-in."

"Don't tell me there's a third closet?" Turning to the opposite wall, her hand reached the knob seconds before Chase's fingers folded over hers.

"Oh," he said softly, "sorry."

"No problem." Her gaze locked with his, his hand remained clasped over hers. She should have said something, moved out of the way, pulled her hand back, anything. A simple blink to break the invisible connection would have helped, but she was rooted to the floor and had a hard enough time breathing, never mind thinking.

"I, uh…" Chase rocked forward and for a split second she held her breath, thinking he would kiss her again. One thought prayed, *yes please*, and the other screamed *not again*. As her eyes drifted closed in anticipation, his hand lifted from hers and he took a wide step back. "Should let you open the door."

"The door?" She blinked. "Right." Turning the handle and sucking in a deep breath, she steadied herself and pulled open the door.

Chase's eyes instantly narrowed, mirroring her confusion. "Is that supposed to be in the master?"

"Every house I've ever been in, the heating and air units are usually in a hall, sometimes in the garage or occasionally in the attic, but no, never in a bedroom."

"I'm not an expert on forced air—"

"We just call it central air."

"Okay, central air, but this one looks older than I am."

"Probably is." Grace closed the door. "Remember, this place hasn't been lived in for at least ten years. Maybe more."

Chase nodded and took a step back, opened the other two closets again, then turned to face Grace. "I bet if we put a unit in the attic and turn that into a closet, we could have a small master bath put in."

"Oh, that would be great." Grace scurried over to the second closet and, standing inside, used her hands to measure out the distances. "This one might be a bit tight, but it's still a good size closet." She closed the door and crossed the room to the first one she'd seen. "Yep. This would be the one. Room for a nice sink, and a decent shower." She closed the door and spun around. "Where's the main bathroom?"

Chase shrugged. "Must be off the hall somewhere."

"You hope. We might have to look for an outhouse and a steel tub on the back porch."

"Not in this lifetime." He chuckled, and lightly placing his hand at the small of her back, nudged her out of the room.

With the door open wide, she could see a huge bathroom. "This is your lucky day."

"Why?"

"The bathroom backs up to the big closet and..." She turned in the middle of the room. "Oh my God. Look at that tub."

"Needs a shower."

"Shower?" A claw foot tub big enough for Sasquatch to soak in and this guy was thinking shower. "This is fantastic." Without a moment's hesitation, boots and all, she climbed into the tub and leaned back. "Oh yeah, definite heaven. Tub has to stay."

When she opened her eyes and looked up, Chase stood legs slightly apart, arms crossed, smiling down at her. "Guess we're keeping the tub."

● ● ● ●

If he'd been unsure before, there wasn't a lick of doubt in Chase's mind now. He wanted this house very much. And he wanted Grace Farraday too. Not just the way a man wants a beautiful woman. This was about more than getting into her pants. This was about curling up on the sofa with your best friend on a cold night with a hot cup of tea. About sharing the last piece of breakfast toast because someone forgot to run to the store for a fresh loaf. About sharing the good, the bad, the big, the small, with that one special love of your life.

Love of his life? Was Grace the love of his life? A woman he'd met less than a week ago? A woman who wanted to slay dragons and conquer cities. Big cities. A woman who wanted to be anywhere except here in Tuckers Bluff. A woman who didn't seem to have one blessed life goal in common with him?

"Come on." Grace lifted herself from the tub and climbed out. "Let's check out the rest of the house. Even if you've already made up your mind."

"Who said I already made up my mind?"

"You mean besides when you said all it needed was a little love?"

"Maybe I meant someone else's love."

"You could have, but you didn't." Skipping the third bedroom, she doubled across to the kitchen. "Hell, you even got excited about these lopsided old metal cabinets."

Was there any point in debating her? "Don't you think I should at least sleep on it?"

"I think you should go back to New York and really enjoy your life, but what I think doesn't count for much lately."

"Sure it does. I'm keeping the tub."

Grace let out a smile and laughed. "Pretty generous of you considering the house isn't yours."

He looked over the kitchen, with surprisingly large windows, and pictured a little updating. Replacing a few cabinets, something traditional and fitting with the architecture and light. After years of living in the shadows of Manhattan's skyscrapers, he realized he liked light. Lots of it. Out the back door he stepped onto a porch almost as large as the front of the house. Crossing to the railing, he kicked something that noisily slid with his foot. "What—"

"That's a dog dish." Grace maneuvered around him and leaned over to pick it up. "No way this has been here for ten or more years."

Each glanced off into the distance, scanning the barren land as far as they could see.

"Who else lives around here?" he asked.

"You mean like someone you could run across the street to and borrow a cup of milk or a dish of dry dog food? No one." She set the dish back down and froze. "Did you hear that?"

Chase nodded. "Sounded like a growl."

"Is it my imagination, or did it sound like we're standing over it?"

Shaking his head, Chase reached over and, gently folding his fingers around her arm, pulled her slowly back into the house. "I think we've seen enough for today. When we get to the car I'll give Adam a call."

"DJ too."

"DJ too. One or both of them can come out and see if they can find what's growling at us. If it's an injured animal, we don't want to get too close."

"But the food? Did you see a bag of dog food anywhere?"

Chase slid his hand from her arm to around her waist and circled her around. Leaving his hand at her back, he nudged her forward. "No, and I'm not going to look now. Whatever it is, we'll figure it out later."

No reason he couldn't add mysterious growls and twenty-year-old dog dishes to his growing list of things he needed to figure out—and fast.

CHAPTER FIFTEEN

"**Y**ou don't suppose it has something to do with the stray do you?" Aunt Eileen asked over the rims of her cards.

Ruth Ann discarded two. "Maybe the construction crew has been feeding whatever it is?"

"That makes no sense at all." Dorothy held her cards against her chest. "There hasn't been any real work at Brooks' place for weeks. If the carpenters won't drive to Tuckers Bluff for a day's work, who the hell is going to drive all this way to feed the dog?"

"If it's a dog," Sally May added.

"What else would it be? No one feeds dog food to wild animals." Dorothy went back to rearranging her hand.

Sally May's expression contracted as though she'd just bit a lemon. "My niece in Dallas feeds the raccoons."

"Well your niece in Dallas is one pet away from an official title of Crazy Cat Lady," Aunt Eileen softened her words with a smile.

Grace studied her own cards, but her heart wasn't in it. Last night, when her aunt had insisted that she needed a ride into town to play cards because the tendonitis in her ankle made driving painful, Grace resisted calling out hogwash. For as long as she had shared a home with her aunt, the woman had never once mentioned the words *tendon* or *itis* in the same sentence, and even fewer times had she not considered herself fit to drive anywhere in any vehicle at any time. But Grace had also been intrigued at the thought of escorting Chase to see the old foreman's house. Now that she'd gotten her senses fired up by a mere heart stopping glance, and anxiety blooming with concern over a lost stray, she was just plain glad for the distraction. Even if playing cards with the ladies wasn't working out so well. "I just wish DJ had been at the station when we got back."

"But he said he'd stop by on his way into town. That he'd be driving right back and it wouldn't be long," her aunt reassured. "I'm sure whatever it is, he'll figure it out."

"I suppose." Grace looked at her cards a second time, suddenly noticing she held a hand of hearts.

"How many cards you going to want?" Dorothy asked her.

"None. I'll play these."

Four slightly slack-jawed heads looked at Grace, then each other, and four sets of cards landed face down on the table with echoes of "I'm out" bouncing off each other.

"What have you got?" Sally May asked.

Grace grinned. "No one anteed up, I don't have to say."

"You want to live to see another sunrise, you'd better not pull any of that prissy lawyer malarkey." Aunt Eileen skewered her with one of those motherly stares that Grace hadn't seen in a long time.

"Sorry. I couldn't resist just a little teasing." Grace leaned to her side, kissed her aunt on the cheek and laid down her cards face up. "Five hearts."

Over the next few rounds, she and her aunt took turns winning the pots. If all the games she'd played with the Tuckers Bluff Ladies Afternoon Social Club since she was a teenager had been for real money, Grace would have probably paid for law school twice over by now.

"I wonder how much longer before Chase and Brooks talk money?" Aunt Eileen grabbed a couple of chips and tossed them into the pot. "I mean," she turned to Grace, "you seem pretty sure he wants it."

"Every trial lawyer wants jurors as easy to read as he was. Yeah, I'm sure." If she was honest with herself, she'd have to admit by the time they'd meandered into the hall bath, even she'd fallen in love with the dilapidated old house. "My guess is as soon as Brooks is finished with his last patient, Chase will be waiting."

"Apparently," Ruth Ann lifted her chin and pointed toward the front door, "sooner than that."

Brooks, Toni, and Chase came in the front door. His hand across his wife's lower back, Brooks led Toni to the opposite end of the Café. Chase turned toward the card-playing ladies.

"Or maybe not," Aunt Eileen muttered.

"Good afternoon ladies." Too damn good looking for his own good in crisp jeans and a button-down shirt, Chase came to a stop at Grace's side.

Try as she might, she couldn't quite make out what the situation at hand was. His smile was bright and pleasant, but his eyes lacked the twinkle they'd held earlier today. Her heart tightened in her chest and she found herself hoping above hope that Brooks hadn't said no to Chase. She knew how much he wanted the house, and that was reason enough for her to want it for him too.

He leaned over and faced her. "If the game can spare you, would it be considered conflict of interest for you to offer a little legal guidance?"

With four pairs of eyes staring at her, Grace wasn't quite sure what to say. Turning, she glanced over her shoulder at her brother and sister-in-law. Toni waved, but it was Brooks who, with only the hint of a smile and a dip of his chin, gave her the answer she needed. "We'll have to see."

The twinkle in his eyes returned and she couldn't help smiling back at him. That blasted sparkle was seriously growing on her.

• • • •

There were a lot of things Chase had done in his lifetime that made no sense. To many, giving up a lucrative Wall Street career to buy a small feed store in the middle of West Texas was beyond insane and certainly qualified as making no sense. Yet, as surely as he'd known that was the right move, he knew having Grace at his side for this discussion was critical. And if there was one thing Chase had learned early on in business dealings, it was to trust his gut.

Chase waved an arm towards Brooks and his wife as she eased her chair away from the card game. "Shall we?"

Only the slow and slight bob of her head told him that she was less than comfortable with the situation he'd just put her in. But the thing that tickled his interest most at the moment was that in only a few days he was confident he'd learned to read her fairly accurately. It was almost laughable. For all of his adult life he'd considered women an enigma to be accepted, not understood. Who knew a country gal at heart with fire in her soul would be so easy for him to figure out.

"Have you talked money yet?" Graced asked softly once they were out of ear shot of the gaming table.

"A little."

Still walking, she didn't slow her pace but shot a curious sideways glance his way. Maybe he wasn't reading her quite as well as he'd thought.

"Isn't this fun?" Hands resting on her well-rounded belly, Toni beamed at Grace's approach. "We just couldn't figure out what to do with that place and here Chase turns up and solves our problems."

Sliding into her seat, Grace's brows folded into a deep-set V. "The house was a problem?"

"Not a problem." Brooks looked at his sister and squeezed his wife's hand. "More of a loose end."

This casual way of doing business was something Chase could easily get used to. No hardball negotiations. No misleading half-truths. Though he doubted he was going to be having a lot of opportunity to do any more buying or selling once they agreed on a price. He had his business and soon his house. That would be it for him for a while.

"In all fairness to full disclosure," resting his arms on the table, Brooks steepled his hands in front of him, "construction crews are not easy to keep in these parts."

Chase nodded. They'd already had this discussion in reference to the hospital project, so he'd figured as much out without need for repetition, but then again, this was business Texas style.

"How handy are you with a hammer and saw?" Brooks asked, a little too earnestly for Chase's liking.

"Not very. I'm better at computers and spreadsheets."

"Then a fixer-upper may not be in your best interest." Grace looked up at him. "Not unless you have an entire family of handymen willing to swoop down and help."

"Only child." He smiled. "But I'm sure I could learn."

Brooks stared at him intently, then glanced from his sister to Chase, nodded his head and smiled. "I bet you can."

"Now that that's settled." Chase retrieved the folded paper from his breast pocket. Opening it up, he smoothed out the folded creases and laid it out in front of Grace. While Brooks was finishing up with his last patient, Toni and he had chatted in Brooks' office. She'd mentioned a price. He'd scribbled that across the top like letterhead. Notes and thoughts from the conversation on the right, he'd bullet-pointed calculations and decisions on the left.

"When did you do this?" Having already given the page a quick perusal, Grace looked over the writing once more.

"Waiting for Brooks."

Not lifting her head, she turned to face him. Her eyes met his and one corner of her mouth tilted up in a smile. "You sure you need me?"

He simply nodded and, retrieving a pen from his pocket, set it in front of her.

Once again she glanced at him without lifting her head, but this time the smile reached both sides of her mouth. She lifted the pen, checked price, time, circled land, and under where he'd written inspection reports and estimates, she added option time and money then penciled in beside it *fourteen days*, *one hundred dollars*, and once again, tilting her head towards him, raised her brows in question.

Chase nodded. He'd thought about it, but hadn't nailed down time and money.

Squinting up at the ceiling, she tapped the pen on the table, then looked to her brother. "Would you say the house is set about two hundred feet from the road?"

"Could be. Maybe a little more."

Grace nodded. "Bet it's more like three hundred."

"Some of my favorite people." Abbie set a glass of water in front of each person at the table. "It's too early for dinner and judging by the serious look on everyone's face, I'm going to guess this is business which calls for a slice of Frank's pie."

Fingers still splayed on her tummy, Toni leaned forward conspiratorially. "What is it today?"

"He was feeling ambitious." Abbie smiled, "Key lime and banana cream."

"Oh, I love banana cream," Toni practically moaned.

Brooks chuckled, kissed his wife on the cheek and turned to Abbie. "We'll share a piece."

"Spoil sport." Toni smacked him lightly on the arm, then shifting her attention back to Abbie added, "I'll have some green tea with that too, please."

As soon as everyone had placed their orders all eyes returned to the paper Grace held.

"So, what are you thinking?" Brooks asked her.

She scribbled to one side. *Single lot 3 acres 200 by 600*. Then added *or Double?*

Hefting one shoulder he gave her a casual shrug. His math was good enough to figure out that she was doubling the depth from the road, but had no idea why she asked for the second. "Which would you do?"

Without hesitation, Grace tapped at double.

"Okay. If you say so."

"Me?" Her brows shot up. "It's going to be your house."

"True, but the sign of a good businessman is not just bringing in good advisors, it's doing what they say."

"Very well." Grace looked to her brother. "Tomorrow, you'll have a signed letter of intent. And then we'll go from there."

Brooks reached out to shake Chase's hand. He was getting to like these handshake deals. But even more, what he really liked was that Grace had just said *we*."

CHAPTER SIXTEEN

Considering how excited Grace was to draw up the initial paperwork for Chase's new house, anyone would think she was the one who was going to buy it and move in.

"Thanks for the ride, Pussy Cat." Aunt Eileen hurried into the kitchen. "It's been nice having you home to join us again."

"My pleasure." It had been a long time since her aunt had called her by that particular pet name. She'd been a freshman in high school when she'd informed her aunt that if she was too old to be called Gracie, Pussy Cat was even worse. Back then it hadn't taken much for her to be embarrassed and being called Pussy Cat in front of her friends and classmates had more than done the trick. It took her aunt a while to break the habit, and even after all these years, once in a while the name slipped out. Like now. And like a broken-in pair of favorite slippers on a chilly night, the feeling was familiar, comforting, good. "What's the plan?"

"For what?" Standing in front of the oven, Aunt Eileen turned the knob.

"For what what?"

Pulling the foil off the large casserole, Aunt Eileen slid it past the open door and turned to her niece. "Is this a trick question? You asked me what's the plan?"

"Oh." She hadn't realized she's said that out loud. For three years her plans were laid out and clear. Get a JD and MBA at one of the best universities with a networking system mere mortals envied. With an income worthy of her education and completely unrelated to and non-dependent on four legged animals, she'd be able to go places and do things that most people only dreamed of. Find out firsthand for herself how much of single life in a bustling big city lived up to the hype. "I, uh, meant about supper."

Aunt Eileen closed the oven door. "Same as every other card playing day."

For as long as Grace could remember, her aunt made casseroles and other dishes to heat and serve after a day of card playing. Some of the crazy things she'd come up with were still Grace's favorite, like the tuna and potato chip casserole.

"Aunt Eileen," Little Stacey bounced through the back door, "Mommy said I can't do the Pee Wee rodeo this year."

"She did?" Aunt Eileen leaned over just in time to catch the child in a bear-sized hug as the crocodile tears streamed down the munchkin's face.

Grace could see her aunt biting her tongue. She would never contradict the child's mother.

"She thinks I'm still too young. Said maybe next year."

"Well, that's not so far away." Aunt Eileen plastered on a bright smile.

The screen door squeaked open seconds before Catherine pushed her way into the kitchen. "It's going to be one of those days."

"Daddy says I'm older than Aunt Grace when she started."

"Yes, sweetie." Catherine squatted by her daughter and brushed a stray lock of hair behind her ear. "But things were different for Aunt Grace."

Rather than address her mother, Stacey pulled away from Aunt Eileen and turned toward Grace. "Different how?"

More than anything Grace would have preferred to stay out of this conversation. Looking to her sister-in-law, she silently pleaded for Catherine to answer.

"Sweetie." Catherine got the message loud and clear. "Remember, your Aunt Grace started riding on her Grandpa Sean's saddle when she was a baby. By the time she was your age she'd been riding for a lot of years."

Staring at Grace, Stacey stood perfectly still, sucking in her lower lip. And then let it go. "I won the ranchathon."

"You did, baby, and you can do it again next time, but the rodeo is for little girls and boys who have been doing this a long time."

Grace didn't have the heart to tell Catherine there was little difference between the family ranchathon and the junior rodeo. Though she desperately wanted to encourage Stacey. Growing up, Grace's favorite thing in the world were the horses, and training for the competitions and winning gave her the confidence she would later need to shine through seven years of academic competition.

"Will you teach me?" Intense blue eyes bore into Grace.

"I, uh..." She glanced at Catherine, who seemed to have her own words stuck in her throat. Aunt Eileen on the other hand was grinning like the Cheshire Cat and nodding her head. "I won't be here very long. Remember, after Uncle DJ's wedding I'm going back to Dallas?"

"Then you'll have to start now." Stacey latched onto Grace's hand and tugged.

"Stacey," Catherine started, "Aunt Grace—"

"Thinks that's a great idea," Aunt Eileen chimed in. "Dinner won't be ready for a while and sunset is still a ways off."

Apprehension glistened in Catherine's eyes. Weren't they all one hell of a set? No one wanting to contradict the other one. Grace needed to find a way to gracefully get out of this mess and let everyone off the hook. Too bad the only words that came to mind were, "It's better to start fresh in the morning."

The next thing Grace knew, she had fifty pounds of delighted child in her arms and a whole new agenda for the rest of her time in Tuckers Bluff.

• • • •

For the better part of an hour, Chase checked his computer or pretended to read the paper. When he wasn't doing either of those, he was pacing and debating calling Grace. After leaving the café,

Grace promised to have a letter of intent in his mailbox tonight. She didn't specify when tonight, and though he wasn't necessarily anxious to see it, he was looking for an excuse to hear her voice. And didn't that make him feel like a crushing teen. All he needed to do now was turn her combination lock around or leave flowers on her desk.

Crossing the room and stopping at the window, Chase tried to remember the last time he'd had a woman crawl so deeply under his skin. No one he could remember since the sixth grade when he'd fallen head over heels for Debbie Brown and her blooming figure. He'd lost interest a few days later when his dad bought him a new baseball bat. His mom used to say, *What separates the men from the boys is the price of their toys*. Wasn't that the truth. This new—or old—house was going to cost him a hell of a lot more money than every bit of baseball gear he'd ever owned. Only he didn't see his interest in Grace waning, no matter how many toys he bought.

Which brought the same nagging question to mind. What was he going to do about it? The woman had made it perfectly clear she wanted none of the things he did. Or did she? The way she laughed when they were out riding, or beamed while taking in the details of the house. No matter what he'd told Andy, he'd felt like they were indeed hunting for their new home. More than once the word "we" had slipped out and she never corrected him. So was she as hell bent on spreading her wings as she claimed?

His cell phone sounded and Chase practically leapfrogged over the side chair to the ringing phone on the nightstand. "Hello?"

"Hi." Grace's voice washed over him like a soothing ocean breeze.

"Hi." *Smooth Prescott. Smooth.* "This is a pleasant surprise."

"I wanted to let you know I just shot the LOI your way. It should be in your email by now."

His phone at his ear, he settled into the easy chair he'd practically vaulted over a moment ago and fired up his laptop. "Yep. It's here."

"Good. I'll need you to look it over before signing it."

"Always do." Though tonight he'd been so distracted he'd probably have to look it over twice. "You sound tired."

She drew out a yawn. "Long day. I don't have enough practice keeping up with kids."

"Kids?"

"My niece Stacey. She wants me to teach her to barrel race," she chuckled, "like yesterday."

"Patience, a youngster's best virtue," he teased.

"Add that to a nervous mother and I had my hands full tonight."

Leaning back, he lifted his feet onto the ottoman and closed the laptop. Business could wait. "What do you mean?"

"Well, Catherine isn't, shall we say, fond of horses. The idea of her daughter learning to barrel race isn't top of her list. Even though the kid did really well in the flag races earlier this year."

"Dare I ask what that is?"

"Minor competition in fun. Kids ride from barrel to barrel and grab a flag, then put it back. Basic stuff."

"I see." He didn't really, but he was enjoying the sound of her voice.

"Anyhow. After a glass of wine and repeated explanations that at her daughter's age no one was going to be flying around barrels yet, we seemed to have Catherine onboard with giving Stacey some training."

"Who is we and what kind of training?"

"We would be most of the Farradays at dinner, and the training starts with horsemanship. Caring for a horse. My brother has been doing a great job with that part, but there's a lot to learn. How to use her hands and legs, timing, conditioning consistency, and how to maximize the potential of her horse. It will take years."

"I gather you didn't tell her that?"

"Nope." Rustling sounds carried through the line and he figured she was getting comfortably seated too.

"From what I've heard, she'll have the best teacher."

She blew out a sigh. "Just because I used to be a good rider—
"

"Those trophies in that cabinet say better than good."

"The key words here are *used to be*. None of that means I can teach. Besides, Aunt Grace won't be around long enough to teach all she has to learn."

He held back a sigh, not really wanting to be reminded of her short timetable.

"Aren't you even a little enthused to share your wisdom with Stacey?" At her long pause he braced for a response he didn't want to hear.

"Maybe just a little."

The smile in her voice left him grinning from ear to ear. *A little* he could work with. He just needed a running start. "I owe you a dinner."

"You don't have to—"

"A bet is a bet."

Something akin to a giggle came through his phone. "Okay. But you'd better be warned, the two of us having dinner at the café will have tongues wagging all over town."

"I didn't have the café in mind."

"Oh, well," she laughed a bit louder, "if you're planning on driving all the way to Butler Springs, then you'd better expand the tongue wagging across the county."

"I can handle it. Can you?"

"Ha! I'll be gone soon. You're the one who gets to live here and deal with it." Her words were a little harsh, but her tone was still filled with humor.

"No worries. What are you doing Friday night?"

"Can't. Monthly girls' night is going to be last minute wedding details. Not sure if it's jewelry or favor making."

"Okay. What about Saturday night?" He crossed his fingers. If he waited until after the wedding next week, it might be too late.

"I think I can make that work. But if I have to cancel last minute because of some crazy maid of honor duty, don't take it personally."

"Deal."

"Hope you know what you're getting into."

He could say the same thing to her. "I'm a big boy."

"That's what they all say," she taunted.

The rumble in his chest burst forth in a blast of laughter. If he could pull his plan off, life just might turn out to be way better than good.

CHAPTER SEVENTEEN

"**O**ne more time. Please?"

Three fifty-five. If Grace didn't get Stacey off the horse soon, she'd either be showing up to girls' night smelling like a barn or late. Neither option appealed to her. "Five more minutes and that's it."

Behind her, the sound of Finn chuckling grew closer. "You were the same way."

"Impossible. No one is this tenacious," she called over her shoulder.

"That's what you think." Finn came to rest beside her. "She's as good as you were too."

"You're not old enough to remember that."

One foot on the lower fence board, Finn rested his arms over the top coral board. "When your kid sister rides a horse better than you do, it's hard to forget." Pulling back, he slid an arm over her shoulder. "Of course, I got over it when it turned out I could rope a steer and you couldn't."

"Not couldn't. Didn't want to." She patted his hand. "I haven't said a word to her yet about using her legs, and yet, she does it by instinct. If I didn't know better I'd swear it was genetic."

"Her grandmother did have more trophies than you and I put together."

"Makes you wonder about the longtime argument, nature or nurture."

"Not me. Never argue with Mother Nature." Slipping his arm at his side, he climbed into the coral. "Go on and get ready for tonight. I'll take over horsemanship 101."

"You're a prince." She looked over at Stacey walking the horse in their direction. "Uncle Finn is going to take over."

Stacey nodded and flashed a toothy grin. If Grace had expected her new niece to be unhappy at her leaving early, Grace would have been sadly disappointed. As long as she was on or near a horse, Stacey couldn't be happier.

"How's it going?" Joanna, Finn's fiancée, strolled up.

"Great. Finn's taking over. I just need few minutes for a quick shower. Do you know if everything's ready to go?"

"Yep." Joanna turned and began walking with Grace at her side. "If I understand correctly, the ladies social club has skills besides poker playing. From the looks of it, we may be up all night and covered in glitter."

"That sounds about right. Just remember the cake balls are boozed. Don't overdo or you may wind up glued to the favors."

"Got it."

They'd made it within a few feet of the back door when Grace's cell phone rang. By now she recognized the number. Last night after supper Chase had called to update her on the paperwork, confirmed they were still on for Saturday night, and somehow they'd wound up talking about everything and nothing for almost an hour. "Hello."

"How'd it go today?" Chase asked.

"About the same as yesterday. I don't think I'm supposed to feel old before thirty but let me tell you, this kid has one heck of an energy level."

Joanna signaled she'd wait for Grace in the house.

"Someday someone is going to find a magic pill to recreate that energy and get very rich."

"Amen." She glanced toward the house. It was getting late and she needed to hurry, but just like last night and the night before, she didn't want to end the call.

"About tomorrow night?"

"We're still on."

"Good. Don't wear blue jeans."

She spun around and leaned against the back door. "Ah, we have a dress code."

"If you really want to, you can wear jeans, but—"

"I only wear jeans here at the ranch. I'm sure I can find some old thing to toss on."

The screen door squeaked open and Joanna popped her head out. "I'm really sorry," she whispered pointing to her watch.

"Sorry, but I have to run," Grace said. "See you tomorrow."

"Four o'clock."

"A little early for dinner but I'll be ready. Four p.m. sharp."

"Have fun tonight, but don't get tipsy and forget where you live."

"Har har har. Till tomorrow."

"Tomorrow."

The phone dinged with a disconnect and she wished they could have chatted just a little longer. It wasn't doing her any good to wallow in the upcoming loss of his company, and she'd already made peace with ignoring her instincts and not staying away from Chase Prescott till she could escape Tuckers Bluff, alias Mayberry, after the wedding. What she couldn't make peace with was how much she'd miss these conversations once she'd returned to Dallas. And wasn't that a bit of a problem?

• • • •

"Glad you're back early." Meg looked up from the kitchen island at Chase. "There's been a last minute change of plans."

"How's that?" He pilfered a cookie from one of several plates piled high with freshly baked goods. "Anything you need my help with?"

"Not unless you want to be up to your eyeballs in wedding plans." Adam walked into the kitchen and, heading directly for his wife, planted a quick, firm kiss on her lips before taking a cookie for himself and facing Chase. "I suggest you join me in our apartment upstairs. Our fridge is stocked and the TV has a ball game with our name on it."

"Wedding plans? For Becky and DJ?" Chase asked.

Meg nodded. "So many folks want to help that we had to move tonight from Becky's to here. We've got more space than her apartment."

Chase accepted a beer Adam handed him. "I see what you mean." He started to decline the invitation and quickly decided the distraction, and distance, would be better than sitting alone in his room pretending not to hear the people downstairs. One in particular. "Thanks."

"Hey," Adam said over his shoulder, "we men have to stick together."

Beer in hand, Chase followed Adam up the stairs, resisting the urge to check behind him for the early arrival of the women.

"I hear the sale of the foreman's property is locked down?"

"Yeah." Chase nodded to Adam's back. "Survey's been ordered. Documents have been sent to the title company in Butler Springs."

"Brooks tells me that y'all are thinking you can wrap this up in the next couple of weeks."

More like one, but it was all dependent on the survey. Newly divided land was a little different than reading existing meets and bounds. "Pretty much."

The front door downstairs must have opened because a multitude of definitely female voices carried up to the third floor. From the way Adam studied him, he was pretty sure he'd gotten busted listening.

"You like my sister."

It wasn't a question, but he nodded anyhow.

"We've been known to be very protective of Grace."

He could imagine. A little too vividly.

"Aunt Eileen always said a girl will expect to be treated the way she's treated at home."

"Makes sense." Chase didn't have any sisters but the old adage children learn what they see, not what they hear, came to mind.

"We weren't allowed to get away with any teasing or disrespect. No locker room talk in the house."

That wasn't surprising. From what he'd seen of the Farraday home, they had to be the only non-dysfunctional family in the country.

Heavy footsteps stomped up the steps to Adam and Meg's private apartment. Too many steps for one person. DJ popped in the door first, Brooks on his heels.

"I figured if the girls were going to hang out all night," Brooks set a plate of cookies on the coffee table in front of Adam, "we might as well band together to keep this one out of trouble."

DJ raised a single brow. "You do remember 'this one' is the police chief?"

Brooks shrugged. "Won't be the first time Adam and I have had to keep your ass out of trouble."

"Oh for land's sake, I'm not twelve." DJ set a six pack of Shiner Bock on the table beside the cookies. "So," he sank into the nearest chair and looked to Chase, "you're buying the foreman's house."

It wasn't a question either. Confident bunch these Farradays. Quietly intimidating. Only thing was, Chase wasn't sure if his apprehension came from their air of confidence or the fear spawned by what could happen if they knew the things he imagined doing to their not-so baby sister. "Did you ever get a chance to check out the growling animals?"

DJ nodded. "Went by yesterday. No dog dishes, no animals— growling or otherwise. Whatever was there—if it was there—is gone now."

If? There was definitely something growling under the porch. Then again, he lived in Manhattan, what the hell did he know about the wildlife of West Texas. Maybe it had been a damn family of raccoons for all he knew. Did raccoons growl?

"You move fast." Brooks hiked his ankle onto his knee. "Title company notified me the wire transfer was received. For the full amount."

Chase nodded. He wanted the house deal done, lock stock and barrel, before Grace left for Dallas. Since he wasn't quite sure how much time he had, he was doing his best to move fast with everything.

"The closer says we could make this happen as soon as she gets the survey."

That was exactly what he was hoping for. With a little motivation most title companies could close within five business days no problem, and in Texas, where lawyers weren't required to slow things down with a quagmire of paperwork, he'd hoped the cash deal would light a fire under everyone. So far so good.

Still holding onto the longneck beer bottle, Brooks rested it on the side of his boot. "You move this fast with everything?"

"When I know what I want." He met Brooks' gaze. Something told him this was one more test to show what he was made of. City boy or a man worthy of their sister.

All three brothers looked at him and he did his best not to squirm in place.

"We tend to be a bit protective of our baby sister," Brooks added.

Adam bobbed his head. "Told him that already."

"Good." DJ took a sip from his beer.

"But I didn't show him." A tiny smile teased at one side of Adam's mouth and Chase had this ridiculous feeling that he was about to be hung out the window by his feet.

Brooks and DJ looked him over from head to toe and once again Chase did his best to keep a straight face and hide his sweaty palms.

"Grace would kill us," DJ finally said.

"Hmm," Adam mumbled.

Brooks shrugged. "Wouldn't be the first time."

Chase held his ground, and the brothers' gazes.

"She's complicated." DJ leaned forward, resting his forearms on his knees.

He certainly couldn't argue with that.

"And she's hell bent on leaving the dust of this town behind her," Adam added.

He knew that too.

"But you're still in, aren't you?" Brooks asked.

Without a word, Chase nodded.

Brooks smiled. "May have to change my bet."

CHAPTER EIGHTEEN

Four o'clock couldn't arrive fast enough. The favor making party lasted till midnight and Grace didn't get to bed until well after one. Not that it mattered. She'd been too wound up to fall asleep and once she finally had, she was too anxious to stay asleep.

Her only direction had been not to wear jeans. There were four different outfits on the bed, three of which she'd tried on in the last thirty minutes. Two of them twice. In the end, she settled for a floral pattern broom skirt with a casual dark lavender scoop neck top. Not too bright, not too light, and if she didn't hurry downstairs, she might change her mind for the umpteenth time and try out a few more possibilities.

"It's not dinner with the queen," she mumbled to herself.

"Don't you look nice." Aunt Eileen sat in her favorite recliner, quilt squares scattered about her.

"Thank you. I thought you were further along on that?"

"You're thinking of the blanket we made for Brittany. This is for Brooks and Toni's baby."

"Kind of hard to believe a year ago there wasn't a child in sight and now we have three."

"Almost three," Aunt Eileen corrected. "Once this is done we need to start on a blanket for Stacey."

"Don't you think she's a little old for a baby blanket?"

"Of course she is. Hers will be bigger. More for a twin bed. That's why we decided to do the smaller ones first."

"It's nice that the social club is doing quilts again."

Aunt Eileen lowered the hoop encircled fabric to her lap. "Speaking of nice: Where are you two going tonight?"

"I haven't a clue." Not that she hadn't tried. Last night she briefly invaded the man cave where her brothers and Chase had chosen to hibernate in an effort to coax their destination out of him. She'd gotten nowhere. Then this morning she'd called with the pretext of following up on the house sale and once again failed to get any helpful information from him. "But," she glanced at the clock on the mantle, "we should know soon enough. It's exactly one minute to—"

The doorbell chimed and Grace had to stop herself from running to the door. Anyone would think this was her first date. Ever.

"Do you want me to get it?" Aunt Eileen set the fabric aside and grinned. "You know, make a grand entrance and all."

"Don't be ridiculous." Grace may have rolled her eyes, only because there was no way she'd admit she'd actually considered it moments before her aunt voiced the words. Taking a deep breath and brushing her hands quickly down her sides, she reached for the handle and swung the big oak door open. "Hello."

Chase Prescott stood in the doorway in pressed slacks, a button-down shirt and a navy sports coat that deepened the color of his eyes to the same shade as her aunt's cobalt collection. "You look beautiful."

"Thank you."

"Would you like something to drink? There's fresh lemonade in the fridge."

"Thanks," he flipped his wrist, "but we don't really have time."

"Oh." At this hour she hadn't expected him to be in a hurry. "Let me grab my purse."

Chase nodded as she shuffled across the entry to where she'd set her bag down and, slinging the small leather bag over her shoulder, returned to his side. "Shall we?"

With his hand at her back, Chase led her out the door and she almost tripped to a stop. A while limousine idled in front of her.

"We're going in that?"

Meeting her questioning gaze, he nodded. "I hope it's not too much."

"No." She scanned the luxury vehicle from bumper to bumper. "I've always wanted to ride in one."

This time the one stuttering with surprise was Chase. "You've never been in a limo?"

She shook her head.

"What about prom?"

"Small town, remember?"

"Right." He nodded. "Well then milady, your carriage awaits."

If it had been possible to melt to a puddle, she probably would have. Inside, a champagne bottle chilled in a bucket, soft blue hues lit the interior, and a single red rose rested on the seat.

"Too much?" he asked again.

Holding the rose with two fingers, she took a long whiff and slid into place. "No, but you're making it tough for the next guy to invite me to dinner to compete."

A Cheshire grin took over his face. "That's what I'm counting on."

Little over an hour later, they'd sipped champagne, listened to Sinatra, Michael Bublé, and John Legend, and chatted about everything from favorite colors to college football.

"You never cease to amaze me," he said, shaking his head. "You're like a college ball encyclopedia."

"No. Just an Aggie. Yes, you learn academia as well as loyalty, honor and a host of other valuable life lessons, but a bachelor's degree from A&M wouldn't be complete without a thorough and detailed understanding of—"

"Football."

"Yep."

The vehicle momentarily slowed and then continued past the guard booth and through the gates. "We're at the airport?" Halfway to Butler Springs, the small airport supported mostly helicopters for medical emergencies or ranch supervision. Helos were her brother's thing. She'd flown with him a time or two and felt bad that Chase's grand gesture wouldn't be as grand as he'd hoped.

The limo came to a stop, and Chase climbed out first. Extending his hand to her, she accepted, and like a starlet on red carpet night, gracefully exited the limo, one showy leg at a time. On her feet, she offered Chase an appreciative smile, and glanced around for the helicopter. Only there wasn't one. The only thing visible was a sleek, white, needle nose jet. Private jet.

With the front door—was that what it's called—wide open, and steps leading up and inside, the airplane extended an invitation to someone. She double checked the surrounding buildings. A few bays were open in nearby hangars but no sign of a helicopter. Her gaze drifted back to the private plane and for a second thought whoever was escaping, the only thing missing from the extravagant scenario was a red carpet.

"Ready?" he asked, nudging her out onto the field.

She actually did one more double-take. They were walking straight to the private plane. "We're going to dinner in that?"

Chase chuckled. "Beats driving."

Stunned, she took the last few steps to the plane and climbed aboard. A thousand different questions bounced about in her mind. How could he afford this? How badly was he going into hock for this? Should she let him go through with it? What might the special be if they just went to the café? Or maybe she was about to wake up from a dream any minute.

"Make yourself at home."

Inside, she soaked in the comfortable seating, small tables, and more champagne. "Holy shit."

If this was some crazy ass dream, she wasn't at all sure she wanted to wake up.

• • • •

So far, so good. Even though Grace's expletive the second she stepped into the aircraft caught Chase by surprise, it quickly became clear to him that she wasn't upset but seriously impressed. Score one for the Prescott team.

"We'll be taking off shortly. Take a seat wherever you like."

Standing a few feet away from him, Grace scanned the options and quickly settled for the closest seat. "Am I allowed to ask where we're going?"

"You are, but I don't have to tell you."

One eyebrow arched high.

"Yet." The phone at Chase's side rang. "Yeah, Ted?"

"We're ready for takeoff. Should be smooth skies and sunny and clear."

"Perfect." Ted ran a fantastic operation and Chase knew that everything would be exactly as he requested. Within seconds of hanging up, the small cabin filled with a soft jazz tune from the limited repertoire, the engines roared and the plane sped down the runway and lifted off the ground.

Clutching the armrests tightly, Grace intently watched the ground fall away. "I don't understand how something this heavy can fly like a bird, but I'm glad it does."

"Agreed." Seated across from her, he leaned back and waited for her to lose interest in the view.

"You must fly a lot to have your own plane ready at your command." Grace settled back in her seat, crossed her legs, and shifted her focus from the window to Chase.

"I don't fly much at all, and this is not my plane. Chartered."

"Still, this can't come cheap."

"It's all subjective. To an Arab prince, the cost is a drop in the bucket. To the cashier at the grocery store, not so much."

"And to you?"

"It helps that Ted and I have been friends since rooming together in college, but my budget is definitely going to take a hit this month." He flashed a broad smile in an effort to keep the conversation light. "So what do you think?"

"I think a girl could get used to this." The way her eyes lit up, he knew he'd hit on her dreams and goals.

Now if he could just give them some new perspective.

"Last time I got to travel in an airplane I fell asleep. Not doing that now."

He loved the way she smiled when she was excited about something. There was an extra punch to it, one that struck him dead center, sending shockwaves all the way to his toes.

"How long is the flight?"

Glancing up at the digital clock he did a fast calculation. "Little more than an hour."

"So we're talking ninety minute flight time." She squinted out the window and he could almost read her thoughts.

"If you're going to start mapping the movement of the sun, I'm going to have Ted turn around and take you to the café for dinner."

"Ha," Grace burst out laughing. "I actually considered trying to convince you this was too much and to simply have dinner at the café."

He couldn't help but grin at her. It was nice that she was worried more about him, or his finances, than having a good time or doing something new and possibly exciting. No matter what the rest of the town thought about Grace's ambitions, he'd bet his last dollar that, just like Dorothy in Oz, for Grace there could be no place like home.

• • • •

Never had sixty minutes flown by so fast and yet crept along so slowly. The airplane hummed a bit as the landing gear lowered and Grace tried really hard not to squeal at the fast approaching landscape below. She still had no idea where they were. Chase hadn't dropped a single clue no matter how many ways she'd tried to get him to slip up.

The aircraft jerked from hitting the ground and she gripped her armrests a little tighter, not from fear but sheer energy. Not having to ride an eternity to reach a gate was one of the advantages of a smaller plane in a regional airport. The sooner the plane stopped, the sooner she'd know where they'd landed.

Inpatient, she unbuckled her seatbelt and waited for the plane to roll to a full stop. As soon as Chase pushed to his feet, she sprang up beside him. Extending his hand, she slid hers into his and followed him to the now open doorway.

"Enjoy your visit," Ted flashed her a conspicuously conspiratorial grin.

"I'll text you when we're on our way back."

Ted nodded and returned to the cockpit.

At the bottom of the steps, Chase squeezed her hand. "Welcome to the Big Easy."

CHAPTER NINETEEN

Once again that blinding smile took over Grace's face and lit Chase from the inside out. "Shall we?"

"Lead the way."

Still holding hands, they walked inside the small terminal and out to where another limousine awaited them.

Shaking her head at the luxury car, Grace slowed to a stop. "Oh you are seriously raising the bar for first dates."

"You're on to me." He'd argued back and forth with himself whether to take her to a local dive for the best shrimp po-boys in the state, but in the end opted for a traditional five-star dinner. After all, the idea was to show her the high life. "Hungry?"

"Starved, though I'm not sure if I could eat a bite."

"Oh, I think you'll manage."

He'd instructed the driver to take the longer route through the more scenic portions of the town. Listening to her *ooh* at the tree lined streets with original southern mansions and squealing at the streetcars had already made this the best damned date he'd ever been on. First, second or otherwise.

The limousine came down the multi-laned avenue and turned the corner at a narrow street already showing signs of the picturesque and famed French Quarter before coming to a stop at the tired brick building with a cattywampus wooden gate.

Out of the car like a shot the chauffeur circled the hood to open the door for his passengers.

Chase was the first to exit. "I'll let you know when we need the next ride."

"Yes, sir. And if you're looking for nice spot for after dinner, my cousin Louie is playing at Belle Mere's around the corner from ten to three."

"I'll keep that in mind. Thank you." Facing the entrance, a pang of unease tapped at Chase's chest. Maybe she would prefer simple fare. *No time for second guessing.* He pushed the gate open and followed the tunnel-like brick hall all the way to the open air courtyard and felt his unease drift away at the wide eyed appreciation on Grace's face.

"It's beautiful." Her gaze took in the more traditional French decor blended with a hint of New Orleans Cajun. "You certainly know how to pay your debts."

"Glad you like it."

A petite dark haired woman appeared behind the heavy wooden podium. "Reservations?"

"Prescott."

"Party of two. Yes, follow me."

Holding hands under the open sky, with dim decorative white lights overhead and soft melodies playing in the background, Chase was sure he'd made the right choice.

Grace scanned the surroundings as they made their way to the corner table he'd reserved. "I bet the seafood here is to die for."

"Oh, please don't do that." Arriving at their table, he let go of her hand and repositioned himself behind her chair. "I have a lot more planned tonight."

Beaming up at him, she pushed onto her tippy toes and lightly kissed his cheek before settling into her seat. Halfway through dinner and his cheek still tingled with warmth from her barely-there touch.

Conversation came easily, it always had. She'd moaned outright over her sea bass and he'd had to take a long swallow of ice water to counteract the impact. When it came time for dessert, he politely declined the waiter's offerings, ignoring the surprised look on Grace's face. "We have a lot to see still," he explained

"I can eat dessert anywhere." She rewarded him with another superb smile.

Delicately resting his hand at the small of her back, he ushered her out the way they'd come in. Greeted by a large white carriage with a horse of the same color, Chase waved an arm at the cabby. "Milady, your carriage."

"Oh, this is so cool." She hiked her skirt up slightly and climbed up. "It's official," she looked left then right. "Nothing like the Brady's summer hayrides."

"No. I bet it's not," he agreed, delighted when she snuggled up beside him for the duration of the meandering ride across the French Quarter until the carriage came to its final stop. "I hate to have to say this, but we're here."

"Here?" Grace straightened and glanced around. "Café du Monde!"

"Can't come to New Orleans and not have beignets."

"Dessert," she added.

"Have to satisfy the sweet tooth."

"At the rate you're going, tonight is satisfying a hell of a lot more than a sweet tooth."

Oh he certainly hoped so.

● ● ● ●

This had to be the most amazing date any girl had ever been on. Flying in a private jet, riding in a limousine and a horse and carriage, topped off with five-star dining with a handsome, sweet man. Cinderella didn't have it so good. Grace was sure that at some point she'd blink and realize the whole thing was a dream. Though it would have been nice if the dream hadn't included covering herself in powdered sugar while scarfing down the beignet like a toddler tasting sugar for the first time.

"You up for a little walk?"

"Absolutely. Lead the way."

"You keep saying that and I won't be held responsible for where we end up."

"Promises, promises." If this was a dream, she might as well live it up for all it's worth.

Chase led the way down the street and cut through Jackson Square. "This is one of the most recognized squares in Louisiana. Possibly the country."

"Dallas has some lovely old neighborhoods. Charming houses turned into an arts district or modern residences surrounded by young adults and entertainment galore, but nothing like this." She glanced around. Most folks were busy mulling about the streets outside the park. Feeling free from the constraints of neighbors knowing neighbors and the small town gossip mill, she kicked off her shoes, and hiked up her skirt just far enough to climb into the fountain. "Look at me!" she squealed.

Chase's jaw dropped open and his eyes bugged out. For a second she thought she was about to see the mild-mannered storekeeper morph into the Hulk, but instead his head fell back and he barked with laughter.

"Care to join me?"

He shook his head. "One of us needs to stay legal to bail the other one out of jail."

She bent over and, cupping water in her hands, swung her arms forward in an awkward attempt to splash him, but he sprang back too quickly. "Spoilsport."

In the dark of night, most people walked around the park, not through it. She could see Chase considering his options.

"Chicken," she squawked.

It took only a few seconds for him to slip out of his shoes, tuck his socks in and roll up his cuffs. "If we get arrested *no hablo inglés.*"

This time she burst out laughing and loped around the fountain to the other side. The next thing she knew they were playing an odd rendition of *catch me if you can* and she had no idea why, but suddenly wondered why was she running away. Still giggling from the rush, she shifted her weight left and faked him to the right, except he must have seen the move coming because she almost lost her footing when he wrapped his arms around her.

"We need to get out of here before someone calls the cops," he muttered softly.

Feeling the warmth of his breath on her face, she nodded. "Yeah, I suppose we should."

"Yeah," he repeated seconds before his lips captured hers.

All logic slipped away as she fell into the toe tingling kiss. If they were going to get arrested, this was so worth it.

• • • •

"Jeremiah was a bullfrog." Her head leaning back in the leather airplane seat, Grace sang loudly then laughed, shaking her head, "How did any song with a name like that become so famous?"

"Same way *Lemon Tree* shot to the top of the charts back in the day." Chase had opted to sit across from Grace again. Not very cozy, but the smartest way to keep himself from doing something that would most likely earn him a slap in the face.

From the square they'd walked a few more blocks to Pat O'Brien's, the home of the famed hurricane cocktail. His plan had been to pop into a few different clubs. Hopefully at least one with some lighter jazz and a dance floor, but they'd had so much fun singing at the popular piano bar that the closest thing to dancing they'd done all night had been the too-brief lip lock at the fountain.

"That was only because of the vocal skills of Peter, Paul and Mary." Her eyes drifted shut. He thought she'd fallen asleep when she smiled. "I had a nice time. Thank you."

"Thank *you*."

Yawning, she opened her eyes and lifted her head. "Do you always go to such lengths to take a girl out for dinner?"

"This would definitely be a first for me."

Her eyes narrowed. Either in thought or exhaustion, he wasn't sure which, or which he preferred.

"Then why me?" she asked

"You said you missed out on New Orleans a few years ago."

Her chin dipped. "Yeah, I did."

"The nice thing about Texas being in the middle of the country is it's easy to get anywhere fairly quickly."

"Not that easy. Dallas is a major airline hub and I haven't made it any further than home to Tuckers Bluff in the last three years."

"That's different. You've been in school. Once you settle into a full time job—"

"I'll get two weeks a year for vacation."

"In the corporate world, yes. At least at first. Of course government employees get more vacation time, but that's no way to get rich."

"No it's not."

"And you are in this for the money?"

She blinked. "Part of it."

"And the other part?"

Now she smiled. "The excitement of really living life. Like tonight."

"It's a funny thing, living the fast life."

"How is that?"

"Sometimes it's hard to see the forest for the trees."

Grace crinkled hear nose. "Oh it is way too late, or perhaps too early, to be speaking in metaphors. English please."

"People who grow up in big or famous cities don't really appreciate all the city has to offer. The only times I would go into New York City and do touristy things like visit the Statue of Liberty, the Empire State Building, go to dinner or even attend a Broadway show was when company came to town. Much the same way you hadn't been on a horse in years until you had to show me around."

"Not that many years." She frowned.

"Racing for me that day was as thrilling as any killer deal I ever made. And way better than any night on the town—present night excluded."

Her frown lifted to a warm almost teasing grin. "It has been pretty exciting."

"It's not the place, it's the company."

"You've got me there. I definitely think I had way more fun tonight with you than I ever would have had at a bachelorette party with the girls."

"I'm going to take that as a compliment."

"Please do. It was meant as one."

Her eyes drifted closed and he wished they were sitting close together like on the carriage ride. So many things he wished were easier.

Landing back in Texas had been pretty much the reverse of leaving Texas. The limo had been waiting faithfully for their arrival. Grace had scooted in and this time, unlike the plane, they sat side by side, her head on his shoulder. She'd fallen into a deep sleep almost before she'd had a chance to close her eyes. They'd be back at the ranch long before he wanted, but it was what it was. For the rest of the drive he was going to enjoy the moment. Just in case it turned out to be the last moment he ever got alone with Grace Farraday.

CHAPTER TWENTY

It took all the self-discipline Grace had to keep from falling asleep in church this morning. She knew Chase had walked her to the door and escorted her inside, but that was about all she could remember. She was also pretty sure that if he'd kissed her good night, she would have remembered.

Even now, she wasn't all that sure she hadn't dreamt the whole thing. After all, how many ordinary guys fly a gal to the next state for dinner and a night out. Even if they are pretty terrific. And Chase was definitely ranked high in the terrific department, even if he hadn't taken her to New Orleans for dinner.

"What tractor pull did they drag you through?" Catherine came in the back, her daughter Stacey at her side. "Sorry I missed church. It's been an insane morning."

"What's wrong?" Grace stood dicing tomatoes at her aunt's side.

"Sweetie, why don't you go with—where are the men?"

"Father Tim wants to fix something or other before the wedding next week so Dad and my brothers stayed behind to see how they can help. They should be home soon."

"Oh. Okay." She turned back to her little girl. "Why don't you color in the other room?" Catherine didn't have to ask her daughter twice. Stacey bolted out of the room on a mission. Probably to become the next Pablo Picasso. "It's the new equine therapy program we wanted to do. It's so much more complicated than I'd anticipated."

"But you're a good lawyer," Aunt Eileen looked up from her spot by the stove.

"Litigator, yes, absolutely. But non-profit is not my area of expertise. What little I learned in law school, I've mostly forgotten.

And I do mean little. On top of that there are so many complications. If we reach out to young children we have one kind of problem and if we reach out to adults we have another."

"But you want to do the adult program, don't you?" Grace had seen it so clearly in her sister-in-law's eyes the other day.

"It's too much, between having Stacey home half days until school full-time next year, and handling the business for the ranch end of the ranch—"

"As opposed to the not ranch end?" The question in Aunt Eileen's voice was clear.

"Right. The legal end of the new stable and hiring help to buying horses is keeping me plenty busy."

"Not to mention the little bit of legal work you do for the folks here in town." Aunt Eileen interrupted.

"Exactly. I've been able to file with the IRS for the non-profit status and made the necessary changes for the current project, but that's only the beginning. I could be tied up with paperwork and red tape for the remainder of my natural life."

In the back of her mind, Grace ran through all the conversations since she'd been here discussing Connor's stable, the plans for equine therapy, and the most recent topic of conversation, *Dale*. "Ya'll want this in place to help Dale?"

Catherine bobbed her head. "From what I understand everyone in this family has met Dale at least once."

"At least." Aunt Eileen looked to Catherine. "He tagged along with DJ a couple of times and stayed with us. Very nice young man."

"And DJ wouldn't say what the heck happened, but the undertones of the conversation I heard between him and Connor screamed PTSD."

"Which is what Hannah said equine therapy could work wonders with."

Catherine tapped the edge of her nose. "Give the girl a prize."

"Can I help?" Grace hadn't actually given it any thought, the words just spilled out. She was, after all, technically, a lawyer and all of her classes on non-profits weren't nearly as long ago as Catherine's. Maybe she could stay on an extra week...or two and help set thing up.

"Seriously?" Catherine lit up like the proverbial Christmas tree. "That would be fantastic! The only thing more horrific than setting up this kind of non-profit is running the damn thing. I just can't—"

"Hold on." Grace held up her hand. "I meant some help with the paper pushing until I go back to Dallas."

"Oh." Catherine's face fell almost as fast as Aunt Eileen's. "Yes, sorry. Any help is appreciated. I think DJ wants to go to Dallas to visit Dale after the honeymoon. I don't know what his health will be by then, but from what I've come to learn about my brother-in-law, I'd expect him to bring Dale here to convalesce whether the man likes it or not."

A knock rapped at the back door seconds before Sam, the only cowhand who worked for the ranch, appeared in the doorway. "Sorry to interrupt."

"Sam," Aunt Eileen turned to the door. "I thought you were visiting your girl today?"

"Nope, was on my way to Butler Springs when Officer Reed called my cell. Y'all were still in church. He found one of our cows grazing on the side of the road."

"One of ours?" Grace and Aunt Eileen echoed.

"Yep. Turns out there's a nice chunk of fence down in the east pasture."

She'd almost expected him to say the same pasture where she and Chase had picnicked the other day. "How bad?"

"Not very, but it needs to be fixed and I was hoping to wrangle some help."

Without hesitating, Grace nodded. "Give me five minutes to get into a pair of jeans and we'll go take care of the mess."

"Will do. Thanks, Miss Grace. Want me to saddle Princess for you?"

"That would be great," Grace nodded. A few minutes later and Grace was in the saddle and riding alongside Sam on her way to fix a fence. Talk about a fall from favor. Private jets one night and jeans and cow manure the next morning. They'd nearly made it to the end of the pasture when the downed section of fence came into view.

"Well shit. Excuse me," Sam winced. "I thought I gave it a decent temporary fix. Wonder how many more cows we've lost. I'll meet you at the fence." Without waiting for a response, Sam leaned forward and he and his horse took off like a two-year-old at the Kentucky Derby.

"Here we go again. Come on, Princess." Grace nudged the horse's side. "What is it with all these men thinking they can beat me?"

• • • •

Chase followed DJ into the Farraday house. After church, Aunt Eileen would have no excuses from him for not joining them for supper. So he'd wound up in the little construction pow wow with the good father and the Farradays, and now he was just happy to have another excuse to see Grace so soon after last night.

"House seems awfully quiet," DJ called from the living room, Chase and his brothers on his heel.

"Catherine and Stacey are in the barn," Aunt Eileen wiped her hands, "Grace and Sam went to fix a downed fence."

"Downed?" Finn came around the corner. "Where?"

"East pasture. At least one of the cows is out."

Finn nodded. "I'll change."

"Me too," Connor started when the back door slammed open.

"Oops." Grace came in, slapped her hat at her side and quietly closed the door. "Sam's checking on how many cows got out. I came for reinforcements. Y'all need to turn your ringers back on."

All at once, like an orchestrated chorus line or water ballet, every person standing pulled out their phones, tapped and slid it back in place.

"Sorry," her father was the first to say.

"Connor and I are going to saddle up." Halfway to the stairs, Finn didn't wait for a response.

"What about you?" Grace looked to Chase. "Want to round up a few missing cows?"

He glanced down at his slacks and loafers. "I'm not exactly dressed for it."

"City boy," she smiled.

"Oh shoot." Aunt Eileen snapped her fingers. "This arrived yesterday after you left. Meant to give it to you before church, but it slipped my mind. Probably official looking junk."

Frowning, Grace accepted the envelope from her aunt, her eyes widening at the sight of the return address.

The instinct that always told Chase when to cut the deal and when to cut his losses or when the whole shebang was at risk tightened in his gut.

Moving with unnecessary finesse, every small movement Grace made to open the letter felt like slow motion to Chase and every passing second twisted the knot forming in his gut. For the only time since first pulling into this sleepy Rockwellesque town, Chase realized where he lived didn't matter nearly as much as who he lived with. For him, the only someone was standing nervously in front of him. He didn't know how, or understand why exactly, but in just over a week he'd fallen rock solid in love with Grace Farraday.

Unfolding the section of papers, Grace rapidly scanned the first page. By the time she reached the last line a grin wide enough to span the Hudson had taken over. "I'm in!" she squealed, throwing her arms around her aunt Eileen, the closest person to her.

"That's nice, dear. In what?"

Grace spun around, and threw and her arms around Adam, who had come up behind her to look over her shoulder. "The best international tax firm on the Eastern seaboard."

"What?" Her father reached for the envelope now resting on the table.

"I'm in!" Again she spun around, and this time, threw her arms around Chase.

It took a second for him to swallow the lump lodged in his throat. Slowly his hands lifted to wrap around her waist, then splayed flat against her back, he returned the exuberant hug, sealing the feel of her in his mind. "Congratulations," he mumbled by her ear.

Still in the fold of his arms, she stiffened, gingerly pulled back and, pausing a moment to level her gaze with his, pulled the rest of the way out of his arms and stepped back. "Thank you."

"Would someone please explain?" DJ asked.

Standing stone-faced and rooted to the floor, Sean Farraday handed his son the envelope.

DJ glanced and looked up. "New York?"

"They're the best. I thought since I hadn't gotten any response before graduation that I wasn't in the running."

Adam tugged the pages from Grace's hand, breaking her eye contact with Chase. He wasn't sure what to say, or if he knew how to find the words.

"I thought you didn't want to practice law?" Adam scanned the pages.

Grace's gaze darted to Chase and back. "International would be the exception."

Stunned seemed to be the word of the hour. At least Chase didn't feel left out, not even her family knew what she'd done.

Now Aunt Eileen sidled up beside her nephew and eased the envelope from his fingers. "I don't understand it," she muttered, mumbling something else under her breath about a dog.

Finn's phone sounded. Turning his back to the kitchen, he answered. "Yeah, we got it. On our way." He slid the cell back into his pocket. "Anyone besides Connor and me coming?"

"I'll go." Grace turned to her brother.

"No." Finn shook his head. "We've got it covered."

"But—"

"You should stay," he said softly before rushing off for a quick change of clothes.

Keeping his lips pressed tightly together, Chase desperately wanted to do the same. Ask Grace to stay.

● ● ● ●

How the hell did something so wonderful fall so horribly flat? For weeks after sending in her resume and application, including the recommendation from her international law professor, Grace had been on cloud nine with the possibilities. Her professor and the senior partner at the law firm were old buddies. She'd hoped that would give her an edge. But even after all this time and not hearing back, she hadn't completely given up hope they'd reconsider. Her mind knew it was a lost cause but her heart couldn't deal with that disappointment. So why in the name of all that was holy was she standing in the middle of her kitchen with what should be the best news of her soon-to-be career and feeling like she'd gotten a stocking full of coal for Christmas?

Finn came pounding down the stairs and hurried past everyone. "Don't hold supper."

"Your father's outside already getting the dogs."

The hall bath door opened and closed and DJ came out in jeans. Grace hadn't even noticed him leave. As a matter of fact, Adam wasn't in the kitchen anymore either. The back door slammed open and shut and more pounding feet came down the stairs. Adam too had changed into old work clothes. There certainly were enough closets filled with jeans and shirts in this house to dress an army.

"Better not hold supper," Adam repeated what Finn had already said and hurried out the back door. There was no telling how many cows needed to be rounded up before nightfall.

"I'm going." She yanked her gloves out of her pockets and turned to Chase. "If you want to tag along, I'm sure there's a pair of jeans somewhere that will fit you."

She wasn't at all surprised when Chase nodded. The guy was a good sport. Not a bad horseman either, but definitely a good sport.

"Follow me." Aunt Eileen started for the stairs. "I'll find you something."

"I'm going to saddle up a horse for you," Grace called after them.

Chase nodded and Grace took a step toward the door, stopping to retrieve the employment contract that one of her brothers had set down on the table. The perfect job. Living in the city that never sleeps. Traveling to exciting places around the world. Yes, she'd be working but not even the busiest of lawyers worked twenty-four seven. Close, but not quite. And certainly not if in Paris, Rome or London.

The combination of Finn shouting instructions and hooves beating in synchronization against the hard Texas clay dragged Grace's attention from the all-important letter. Her brothers were off to do what this family did best, take care of each other. Cattle too, but each other. And how the hell was she supposed to do that if she lived half a continent or an ocean away?

"He'll be right down." Aunt Eileen came into the kitchen and pulled Grace into a rib crushing hug. "I miss you already."

"I love you too," Grace muttered through a heavy heart. It wasn't supposed to be like this.

"All ready." Chase flashed a smile that didn't feel very sincere, but at least he was trying.

"The guys are already on their way. Let's go."

"I don't know how much help I'll be. There isn't very much cattle to round up in Manhattan."

"We don't do very much. The dogs do most of the work, but we're probably going to have to scatter in different directions so the more of us the better."

"I see."

"Hopefully, it will go fast."

"Is the whole herd gone?"

Grace shook her head. "But enough to notice." They'd made it halfway to the barn when a fat mouse ran across the path. "I hate it when they…" Her words and steps slowed as a calico barn cat flew in front of her, so close she missed a step.

"Whoa." Chase reached out to steady her. "Guess cats aren't the answer to a rodent problem after all."

He was still hanging onto her arms when another shadow flashed in her peripheral vision, only this one was way bigger than a mouse or a cat. Sure enough, a short distance away a coyote galloped across the land, no doubt after the cat. The circle of life.

"You okay?"

"Yeah, I'm—" All of a sudden Grace was flying backward. Chase's hands circled her waist and she felt herself shift and tumble as he rolled her away from the fall and she came to a stop, he on his back, and her flat on top of him. "Fine."

"Good," he muttered. "What the hell happened?"

To one side, a loud, deep bark answered. She and Chase turned to see Gray standing over them. She had no idea if the animal was smiling or sneering, but when she shifted to get off of Chase, the dog had the nerve to growl at her.

"You'd better not move."

"I'm heavy."

A slight smile lifted one side of Chase's mouth. "Not that heavy."

"That heavy?"

"Okay," his smile widened, "not heavy at all."

"That's better."

Gray took a step back and she'd have sworn he nodded.

"Looks like the hound of the Baskervilles is leaving." Grace pushed up on her elbows.

The shaggy mutt came forward again and with a low rumble, showed his teeth.

"Or not," Chase said, still smiling for some reason.

"Well shit. What are we supposed to do now? Think I can at least roll off of you?"

"You can try." He made an effort at a shrug, but when Grace shifted her weight to one side, the stray inched forward and showed his teeth again. "I don't think so."

"So I just have to stay here on top of you until someone comes out and scares him off?"

Still grinning, Chase seemed to relax a bit. "I could think of worse places for you to be."

"Like?"

His smile slipped. "New York."

"You don't think I'll like it?"

"I think you'll love it, at least for a while. It's me who won't like it if you're there." He swallowed hard, but kept his eyes steady on hers. "Especially if I'm not with you."

"With me?" Her heart did a triple step and all the adrenaline and energy and joy she should have had at the news of moving to New York suddenly began to simmer inside her for a whole different reason. "You want to be with me?"

Chase nodded, his gaze still locked on hers. "Very much."

"Even in New York?"

He sucked in a deep breath and nodded again. "I'd rather have you with me here, but yeah, even in New York."

She couldn't decide what to do or say. But all that excitement that had started to simmer a moment ago seemed to fade away again. "Say that again."

"Even in New York?"

She waited to feel something. Anything. But nothing. "Before that. Repeat what you said before that."

His brows dipped with confusion. "That I want to be with you?"

The rapid beat of excitement and pending adventure tapped against her rib cage. "Yeah, that part. Tell me more."

"About…"

"Don't be obtuse. Us."

Two dark brows shot up high on his forehead, replaced a second later with a smile. Gently nudging her toward him, he eased her head onto his shoulder so she could hear the rapid tattoo of his heart. "I see you soaking in an antique claw foot tub then joining me on the front porch swing to watch the sunset. I see long weekends in cities you've never been and lots of Sundays with the family you love. I see Stacey growing up to be an outstanding horsewoman with the help of her aunt." He squeezed her shoulder gently. "I see a beautiful woman by day, successful at whatever she wants to do, and mine by night."

At the prolonged silence, she lifted her chin to meet his gaze. "You really see all that?"

"And a whole lot more."

Grace's heart had slid from a wild gallop to a comfortable and contented gait. How about that. Her mind raced with stupid closing arguments. Happiness is who you're with, not where you are. Home is where the heart is. And damned if he wasn't right about one more thing. "There's no place like home."

His mouth had barely melded to hers when a tiny voice in the background shattered the moment. "Look Mommy. Just like you and Daddy."

"What the hell are you two doing?"

Grace pulled back and followed Catherine's leather shoe tips up to her face. "I would think that was obvious. We're kissing."

"Yes. I can see that. But why are you kissing on the ground in the middle of the day?"

Though the temptation to shoot back *as opposed to the middle of night* hovered sharp on her tongue, instead Grace lifted an arm to point to Gray. "Because of him."

"Him who?"

Grace looked around, shimmied up and off of Chase and cast a wider net in search of the dog.

Chase pushed upright beside her, and looked around. Not seeing any sign of the dog either, he shifted to face Grace and rested his hands on her hips. "Does this mean you're staying?"

She nodded.

"With me?"

Her head bobbed again.

"For the record, you do know I love you?"

"For the record, I love you too."

She wasn't sure who pulled who first, but she fell into his arms again, her mouth seeking his, or was he seeking her? And none of it mattered.

"Come on sweetie, we need to hurry inside." Catherine's departing steps faded into the background.

"Why are we going so fast? Mommy?"

"Because I want to be the first one to tell your Aunt Eileen the dog won."

EPILOGUE

"I'd never noticed before how adorable the old place was." Grace stepped out of the front seat of Chase's new SUV. "Not that I came around that often, but still, it *can* be seen from the road."

"With the plans she's come up with in only a few days," Chase loped an arm around Grace's shoulder, "I think she missed her calling and should have been an interior designer."

"Don't be ridiculous." Grace rolled her eyes. "Hurry up, we don't have much time before we have to have the guys at the bachelor party and then we need to catch up with Becky and the girls."

Hannah did her best to keep up with her cousin's pace, but Grace was way more eager to reach the front steps. "Catherine says you're going to take over the non-profit after the wedding tomorrow."

"On Monday we're going to sit down together and get me up to speed. Once we've got the direction properly mapped out, the foundation will be my baby."

"I recognize the twinkle in that eye." Ian Farraday, here for the big wedding bash, leaned into his baby sister. "Think Catherine has any idea what she's getting into?"

"Don't be silly." Hannah smacked her brother on the arm. "Determination is an excellent quality in an attorney. Not to mention heading a program like they want, you need someone tough at the head."

"She's that all right." Ian bit back a smile. He loved his cousin, he really did, but as one of the older members of the clan, he had a heap load of memories of a wild and reckless cousin Grace that could make a grown man think twice.

"Truthfully," Hannah shrugged, "I'm not sure either of them know what they're getting into."

"Which is why you'll be here to help."

"I sure hope so." From the first moment the plans to use some of the horse ranch for equine therapy came up, Hannah could barely stop herself from salivating at the possibilities. She loved what she did, but every day more and more people were moving to Dallas and Hannah just wasn't meant to be a city girl.

Ian came to a stop halfway to the house and pivoted to face his sister. "I thought it was all set. You'll be the therapy expert."

"It is. Sort of."

"Sort of?"

"Well. You know me. I don't want to count my chickens before they hatch. Already things have changed from the original vision."

"Yes, but wasn't that because of your input?"

Hannah shrugged. "Some."

"And Connor and Catherine took your advice?"

"Yeah." She couldn't help but smile. She'd been low man on the totem pole for a long while and it felt really good to have someone give her credit for a job well done. And she was good at what she did. Most of it she credited to a combination of a solid education and caring more than she should, some of it to having been raised her whole life around horses, and another big part to how much she loved what she did.

Ian shifted around toward the porch. The empty porch. "Where did they go?"

"Well, from what I've seen with all the cousins I'd guess, *Grace and Chase, sitting in a tree, K-I-S-S-I-N-G.*" Grace didn't even try to hide her laughter.

"Good grief, how did I not catch sooner that their names rhyme?"

"You don't sing enough." Closer to the house, Hannah came to a stop. "Wow. They do say love is blind."

"Grace did say the house was adorable." Ian tilted his head to one side as if that might improve the view. "I hope they're not planning on moving in anytime soon."

"Agreed." One careful step at a time, Hannah tested each wooden stair on her way to the porch. "This sucker does need work, but I guess I can see some charm. Hidden. Somewhere."

Shaking his head, Ian nudged his sister through the open door. "Come on, Pollyanna. Let's find the lovebirds."

"Over here," Grace called out from down the hall.

Following the voices, Hannah glanced from room to room. Maybe she could see the potential. Her adventurous cousin Grace had fallen into tranquil normalcy. An important job, a great guy who obviously adored her, and soon the picture of domestic bliss suitable for *Architectural Digest*. Talk about the brass ring.

"And this," Grace waved her arm, "is what sold me on the house."

"Right," Ian smiled stiffly, "the bathroom."

Under his breath Chase coaxed his soon to be in-law. "The tub."

"And the tub," Ian tossed in quickly. "Great tub. Well done, Cuz."

"Men." Grace turned on her heel and, pausing to kiss Chase's cheek, marched from the room.

Grinning like a lottery winner, Chase shrugged and followed behind her.

Hannah blew out a soft sigh. Every guy she'd ever dated had been nice enough, but never one of those high in the sky firework metaphors applied to her guys. The youngest of her generation of Farradays, she knew she had plenty of time to find the right guy, but all this love-is–in-the-air stuff was starting to make her wonder if anyone would ever make her see stars.

"Penny for your thoughts?" Ian paused on his way to the hall, then doubled back. "You okay, sis?"

"Sure." She plastered on a bright smile and shook her head. "Just thinking. Holy…" Movement in the window caught her eye.

Had her brother not doubled back she would have missed it. Walking to the side, she lifted the glass and peered out. "That's the dog."

Ian came up beside her. "You mean dogs."

"What is taking you two so long?" Grace came back into the room, her hand safely in Chase's.

Just like Grace had said, *first came love, then came marriage. K-I-S-S-I-N-G.*

"Oh my God." Grace ran to the window. "There's two of them."

Chase sidled up beside her. "Well I'll be. That must explain why Finn thought his dog was bigger than ours."

Ours. The mystery dog was theirs? Hannah didn't get the whole matchmaking dog thing. Even now it made no sense. Grace had found her mate and Hannah was here with her brother. *Figures.* All good stories would come to an end before her turn. Then again, what the hell was she thinking? Dogs did not play matchmaker. Life is not a fairytale. And there won't be any knights in shining armor riding up to sweep her off her feet.

MEET CHRIS

USA TODAY Bestselling Author of more than a dozen contemporary novels, including the award winning *Champagne Sisterhood*, Chris Keniston lives in suburban Dallas with her husband, two human children, and two canine children. Though she loves her puppies equally, she admits being especially attached to her German Shepherd rescue. After all, even dogs deserve a happily ever after.

More on Chris and her books can be found at
www.chriskeniston.com

Follow Chris on Facebook at ChrisKenistonAuthor
. or on Twitter @ckenistonauthor

Questions? Comments?
I would love to hear from you.
You can reach me at chris@chriskeniston.com

CPSIA information can be obtained
at www.ICGtesting.com
Printed in the USA
BVHW031142270121
598894BV00010B/63

9 781942 561279